the

Dark Web

Written by: J.T. Withelder

<u>**For Carrie:**</u>

The wind behind my sails,

always pushing me forward.

<u>Burial</u>

When you get to the top, be sure and take a picture.

Allen didn't bother to respond. He knew that they almost certainly would be able to see that he had read the message. Sliding the phone back into the pocket of his blue jeans, he continued on his hike up the mountain.

From the parking area, the top of the mountain was just short of three miles. Most of the walk stuck to the trail which was maintained and easy to navigate. The last half mile or so, Al was forced to veer from the trail and make his own way.

According to the map on his phone, it was a remote location in a small gorge below the peak of the mountain. He hadn't chosen this spot and he would have never known that this area existed. It was chosen for a very specific reason by his employers.

The name he called them was not entirely accurate. He was not an employee in that he was not willingly working for them. Allen was being blackmailed. The incentive was there in the form of a cash deposit of twenty thousand dollars.

The main motivational force behind Allen's hike up the mountain was entirely personal. His life was at stake. He was in jeopardy of losing his family, and everything he held dear.

A few years ago, at the annual company Christmas party, Allen had done something very uncharacteristic of him. After many drinks at the open bar, he and one of the office ladies had slipped into a bathroom and Allen cheated on his wife of twenty years.

To make matters worse, he had set his phone on the counter and recorded the uncharacteristic scene, something that would have never crossed his mind were he sober.

A middle-aged man cheating on his wife is nothing out of the ordinary, he knew but Allen considered himself above the grade. He couldn't tell if it was the booze or bottled up brazenness but he knew in his heart that it was the first time, the last time, and the only time. He regretted it the instant it was over, in defiance of the alcohol present in his bloodstream.

The lady from the office remained silent. Al did not know if that was out of discretion, respect or embarrassment after he had openly sobbed into her shoulder after the deed was done. Without ever watching the video, he deleted the evidence from his phone out of shame before either of them left the bathroom.

He loved his wife fully and completely. They had been high school sweethearts. They had built their life together hand in hand, raising a wonderful son and a beautiful daughter.

If she ever found out about his tryst at the Christmas party, she would be crushed and Allen would end up like so many middle-aged men before him penniless, broken, and alone.

Treading lightly for weeks afterward, Al was sure he would be found out either through the rumor mill or from the woman herself but that moment never came. Weeks turned into months, months into a year, and eventually, the event faded from his memories.

He had almost completely forgotten about that terrible night until a few hours ago when a message appeared on his social media claiming to have something that might interest him.

Allen initially despised the social media wave but having teenage kids had swayed his opinion of the time-wasting sites. Once they had left for college, he had set up an account so he could keep an eye on them while they were away.

He managed to find a few distant family members and old friends from high school so over time Allen learned to take social media with a grain of salt and recognized the positive features of being a participant.

We hope you find this as interesting as we do.

This anonymous message he had received was not one of the positive features. It included an attachment of a video. The cell phone recorded video of him and the office woman having sex. A video of him cheating on his wife.

Allen sat in silence for a long while, unable to comprehend how this still existed. It wasn't until the phone dinged again that he was able to snap out of his anxious fog.

Everything will be fine Allen. Take a deep breath and try to calm down.

Unfortunately, the day had turned into a roller coaster of ups and downs and Allen found himself hovering just on the edge of insanity. The person or persons who had the video of his indiscretion had not alerted him to its existence out of kindness.

They wanted something from him. Something they needed to be done.

*   *   *

The phone dinged again, this time pulling him from the daydream. He was standing in a cramped valley littered with small pine trees. If the trees weren't scattered in such random positions, he would have sworn it was a tree farm.

Looming behind him was a sharp, sheer cliff, hiding the peak of the mountain and blocking the still-rising sun from warming his sweat chilled body. Sliding the phone out once again, he pulled up the messages screen.

Based on your last known position, you should be near the area. Please remember to send a picture before you complete the task.

Placing the phone back in his pocket, he gently slid the tarp-covered load from his shoulders and rested it onto the ground. He stood for a long while, staring at the blue plastic tarp as he tried to catch his breath, wondering if he would be able to follow through with the task.

The work was easy enough but it was the picture that was worrisome. As long as she stayed covered, his mind could pretend it was something else. Sandbags, yard trimmings, or even some roadkill.

Allen knew that if he had to see what was wrapped up in the tarp, his fragile mind would fracture.

Tied to the bundle was a small shovel, which he took from the pile, carefully untying it without unwrapping the tarp. He worked rapidly, sparing no time to neatly pile the dirt or clear the brush from the top. Yet even in his haste, digging the hole took over an hour.

The first few inches of soil were frozen with morning dew and the sharp mountain rocks glanced his shovel every few inches, forcing him to pick around them until they were loose enough to pull out by hand.

When he was finished, he had an oval-shaped hole roughly three feet wide, six feet long, and four feet deep. He didn't know anything about burying a body besides police dramas on television.

He hoped it was deep enough and that the location was so remote that no one would find her until he was also dead and buried. The phone chimed.

We have not received the confirmation photo. Please respond.

Dirt covered fingers smudged the screen of the phone as he punched in a reply.

Frozen ground. Hard to dig. Confirmation soon.

He pressed send and placed the phone back into his pocket with a loud sigh. The next few minutes would test his will and his sanity like nothing else he had ever known or probably ever will know.

He had to be certain he could finish before he even started with the final work. He let out another sigh as he stared at the disturbed ground, not yet able to turn his head to look at the tarp.

Allen wondered who the woman wrapped up in the tarp was and what she had done to deserve such a terrible fate but as soon as the thought crossed his mind, he immediately shut it out.

Thoughts like that would only make things worse and he knew he had very little stability left. He had to get this done while he could still keep his head about him.

Without leaving the hole he had dug, he leaned across the forest floor to grab one corner of the blue tarp and pulled his dreadful package towards the pit.

Using both hands, he positioned it just on the edge of the hole, being careful not to let it overhang too much. The last thing he needed was to end up with this thing on top of him. Once he thought it was close enough, he climbed out.

Standing on the forest floor and out of the hole, he felt more stable somehow. The ground felt solid underneath his feet and it brought some confidence with it, something Allen had been losing at a considerable rate since the start of this assignment.

Squatting down, he drew in a deep lungful of cool mountain air, grasped each corner of the tarp, and rolled her into the grave.

*   *   *

We need you to deliver a package.

Just a few hours before, the task had been presented to him as a way to get rid of the video. In hindsight, he should have realized it wouldn't be something simple but then again, he never would have expected to be in a situation like this in the first place. They sent him an address and told him to leave immediately.

His wife happened to be away on a business trip so there was no need for an excuse. Thinking about her posts on her own social media, Allen wondered if they knew that she was away from home as he grabbed his car keys and headed out to the driveway when his phone chimed again.

Not the car, take the truck.

The message hit him in the chest like a brick. They were watching him. He put the phone away without responding, assuming that they would be able to see him comply with the request. He climbed into the truck, punched in the address they had given him into the GPS on his phone, and left.

The address seemed to be a random house on a random street. Nothing too drab and nothing too special. Just a run of the mill home on a typical street. Following his instructions, he pulled up into the driveway of the home. As he did, the automatic garage door began to open and his phone received another message.

Pull into the garage.

He followed his instructions and the door closed behind him. Glancing at the switch for the garage door, he observed the odd-looking device connected to it.

It was an adapter that allowed the switches in your house to be controlled from your phone. If they could control the switches in a house, they could easily control him.

Turning the truck off, he slowly climbed out of the cab, his work boots making thick clopping sounds as they hit the hard cement of the garage floor. Allen noticed the bundle on the floor and without thinking, he immediately decided that it could only be one thing, a body.

*   *   *

The body in the tarp was now lying in the pit he had dug and he was standing over top of it, a foot carefully placed on either side of the lifeless shape beneath the covering.

With trembling, dirt-covered fingers, he delicately peeled off the taped seam and began to fold the top corners of the tarp, exposing the grayed face of a dead woman.

Her blue lips were closed but her eyes remained open and when he saw her looking at him through her black matted hair, he screamed.

Allen fell backward, onto the woman's wrapped legs and scrambled out of the pit. He rolled out of it, lying on his back for some time, staring up into the bottom bows of the pine trees and trying to forget the horror he had just witnessed in the woman's eyes, wide open but empty. The sun was high in the afternoon sky when he gathered his courage again.

Careful not to look into the pit, he pulled himself up from the ground. Reaching around in his back pocket, he withdrew his phone. Dirty fingers fumbled through applications until he managed to open the camera app.

Feeling with his feet, he shuffled to the edge of the hole and squatted down without looking into it. He held the phone up and took the picture.

*   *   *

We are prepared to make a deposit of twenty thousand dollars in addition to destroying the video of your indiscretion.

That was the response to his message of protest from the garage. He loved his wife and the life that they had built together over the years but taking care of a body was over the top.

Allen was on the fence, leaning towards the side of morality over keeping his affair a secret. There was a human wrapped up in that tarp and he could not bring himself to even think about going near it.

The cash was not the deciding factor and Allen hardly considered it at all. It was a word that they used: *indiscretion.* That word was what got to him. It made him think of how crushed his wife would be.

He thought of his children and how he would have to explain the situation to them. He pictured them sobbing, their eyes welling up with heavy tears. He would never be the man he once was in their eyes. He would never be whole again.

Deciding that thinking about it any longer would only lead to more moral debates in his head, Allen opened his tailgate and grabbed the bundle from the cold concrete floor. It wasn't very heavy and before he could repress the thought, he imagined it was the body of a woman.

The new assumption hovered in his mind as he carefully laid the covered body onto the tailgate and gently slid it into the bed of his truck. Despite the gruesome situation he was in, he still felt the need to be respectful.

*   *   *

Back on the mountainside, Allen wiped the drippings of wet vomit from the corners of his mouth with his coat sleeve. Even without looking at her again, his mind still raced, and just before he thought his mind would finally snap, his stomach did instead.

Dashing away from the pit, he wretched alongside a thin pine tree until heaving only produced bile.

As his sickness passed, he came to the realization that the task was almost done and it brought on calmness once again. He picked up the shovel from the ground where he had left it and spread a layer of earth across the blue tarp.

When he got to the top of the body, he paused for a moment and thought about climbing down into the pit to cover up her face again.

He knew he would be pressing his luck to attempt such a thing. His stomach was empty and his mind was wrought with so much stress that it was numb. Deciding against it, he made sure that the next few shovelfuls of dirt were placed lightly in place rather than just thrown into the hole.

Allen was thankful when she was covered completely but he felt a twinge of regret when he thought about the grains of dirt settling into her open eyes.

*   *   *

Follow the coordinates. You should be familiar with the area.

Allen received the message as the garage door raised without him having to press a button. He had barely read the message before his cell phone's map feature fired up and showed him step by step directions on where exactly he needed to take the body.

Realizing that he had in fact been there before, he wondered how they knew so much about him until he remembered the pictures on his social media.

The area they were directing him to was an area of state gameland that he hadn't visited since he was a teenager. His father took him there frequently to hunt small game and deer.

It pained him to think of such wonderful memories of his dad being tarnished by his current task but it wasn't as though he had a choice in the matter.

His father had passed away, suffering from Alzheimer's at the end of things and now the happy memories of the mountain would be gone for Allen too.

All at once, Allen realized how they knew about his time hunting in the game lands. A picture of he and his dad standing at the entrance sign, holding their shotguns in one hand and a pheasant in the other graced the cover of his social media page.

While he didn't use the site frequently, he did check in on it now and again to keep in touch with long-distance family members and childhood friends. The realization sent a chill down his spine and he wondered what else they would be able to derive from the page.

He followed the directions according to the map on his phone even though he didn't need them. While he drove, he accidentally reached up, almost as an instinct, to turn the map off.

After all, he knew where he was going. Just before he pressed his thumb against the app's "X" button to turn it off, he stopped.

They were tracking him through his phone and he suddenly realized that turning off the map would probably result in a message scolding him for closing out of it so he just let the voice guide him to the already known destination.

*   *   *

In the pine gorge, Allen had replaced the pile of rocks from his dig on top of the layer of earth. He was careful not to throw the stones haphazardly into the hole, deciding that just letting them drop into place was the best option. The only other option was to get into the hole and place every one by hand.

He not only dreaded the thought of getting back into the pit with the body but the sun was just beginning its downward trend in the sky, signaling the afternoon and he wanted to make sure that he wasn't out here anywhere near sunset.

With his pile of stones diminished, Allen continued to work on the remaining pile of earth until it was gone, carefully packing it down into the rocks so that there wouldn't be a large mound when he was done.

Once the area was level with the surrounding ground, he tossed shovelfuls of dirt into the forest around him randomly, hoping to disperse the small pile that was leftover, displaced by the body now four feet under his feet.

Once the pile was gone, he kicked leaves and sticks over the disturbed area and snapped off a low hanging pine bow to drag across the forest floor like a broom. He wasn't entirely sure that he didn't see this in a movie but seemed like a good idea. Just as he was finished, his phone chimed.

We are beginning to become concerned. Please respond with a confirmation.

He tried to send a message back to respond but the phone chimed again.

Error 4301. Service not found.

"Damn it!" he said out loud. Either the mountain was messing up his signal or whoever *they* were had assumed he refused to complete the task and had gone dark. He imagined being thrown to the ground as police swarmed around his truck in the parking area.

While they hadn't specifically mentioned contacting the authorities, the unmentioned threat loomed heavily on his mind. He tried again to send a message to them.

Error 4301. Service not found.

Suddenly filled with an immediate desire to get off of the mountain, he scanned over the burial site quickly and determined that it was indistinguishable from the rest of the forest floor.

He picked up the shovel and began to move quickly in the direction of the trail. The faster he made it down the mountain, the sooner he would know if this ordeal was over or if it had just begun.

*   *   *

"You have arrived at your destination," the robotic voice of the map application told him. He was happy to be able to finally turn off the app, now that he had arrived.

Swinging into the gravel parking area, he pulled into a spot near the forest's edge and put the truck in park before reaching for his phone. Just after he closed the app, his phone chimed.

We see you have reached the parking area. Please go to the following location.

The map reopened without him, switched to walking mode, and a set of coordinates auto-populated into its search bar. It pulled up a picture of the area, which he somewhat recognized. It showed his location in the parking area and a thin orange line that overlapped the walking path that leads up to the peak of the mountain and intersected the Appalachian Trail.

The orange line took a sharp hook to the right a half-mile or so before the final stretch to the top of the mountain, leaving the trail and cutting to a remote area.

Allen studied the map, knowing that the phone signal could get lost as he traversed the mountainside. The location seemed easy enough to get to according to the map. No twists or turns, just a straight line from the regular trail that parallelled the ridge of the mountain.

While he wasn't the best at judging distance, he was familiar with how topographic lines on a map worked and he thought he could use them to find the spot without the map on his phone. He slammed the door closed on the truck and headed behind it to the morbid cargo in the bed.

*   *   *

Shortly after burying the woman, Allen kept at a fast walk as he moved back down the mountain, using the shovel as a hiking stick. He was eager to get reception again but anything more would have been dangerous.

The main trail was mostly clear of smaller debris but the large tree falls and heavy rocks still littered the path, saved by the inefficient process it would take to get equipment this far up to move them.

It was a fast enough pace for him to break a good sweat. As it dried on his skin, he became chilled but he knew the parking area was just a few short minutes away so he did his best to ignore it.

At nearly the halfway point on the trail, he heard his phone chime and his heart leaped in his chest. He had gotten a signal. Allen reached into his pocket and pulled out his phone, hoping that it was another message to confirm that his horrible deed was done.

The thought of being assaulted by police in the parking area crossed his mind again as he moved the phone into view.

Lost your signal. Please confirm that the job is complete.

"Yes!" he shouted into the woods suddenly realizing how quiet it was all around him. Fighting the urge to cry, he maneuvered through the keys on the phone to reply to the message with the picture, knowing that he had to look at the face of the woman one last time to finish the job. He scrolled through his photos back and forth. It should have been right on top of the feed but he could not find it.

Minutes seemed like hours searching through the media on his phone for the terrible snapshot but it simply was not there. His mind was racked with fear and anxiety.

The only conclusion that he could muster was that in his haste and disgust, he never actually pressed the camera button. It was either that or the file had become corrupt.

Either way, he would need to hike back up the mountain. He didn't want to think about the remainder of the task. The hike back up was enough to focus on for now and while he struggled to calm down, he slowly formed the words on the screen to buy him more time.

Bad signal. Not enough to send a picture.

He hoped that it would be enough.

*   *   *

Allen was thankful for the extra rope he always kept in his truck as he wrapped yet another band around the tarp, carefully moving his hands in a way that barely touched the heavy object underneath.

He hadn't been able to fully wrap his head around the task at hand but he understood that it had to be done so he set out to make sure everything went as smoothly as possible for the sake of his own sanity.

He used almost all of the rope to secure the load within the tarp. The thought of the body coming out of the tarp was unfathomable so Allen wrapped it as many times as he could.

When he was finished with the rope, he used what was left of a roll of duct tape from the glove compartment to wrap it yet again, making sure to hit all of the seams where the tarp was folded across itself.

Once he ran out of the tape, he hurried through the cab of the truck and the small toolbox in the bed for something else to secure the tarp. When his hands grabbed a tiny roll of brown twine, he realized that he was procrastinating.

The thin, fibrous string was practically useless for anything besides tying up the recycling and recognizing his hesitation, he threw it back into the toolbox. It was time to go up the mountain, whether he was up for the task or not.

*   *   *

Back at the pine-filled ravine, Allen struggled to catch his breath as well as his scattered mind. The inability to grasp his next task was weighing on him heavily. He needed to dig her back up.

He needed to remove the stones and dirt from her colorless face. He had to look into her open eyes, now pocked with grains of dirt that stuck to the moisture left by the decaying eyeballs.

He felt the urge to vomit again but managed to hold onto his stomach long enough to notice the sun. In addition to the urgency of his employers, the sun was well past its noontime height in the sky and he had no intention of being out here in the dark.

Allen found the place where he had buried the woman's body just a short time before and began to dig, slowly at first but quickening with each shovelful of dirt. Knowing that he only needed to expose her head, he started there.

He made quick work of the already broken up dirt and in just a few short minutes, the metallic clang of the shovel hitting rock resounded in the gorge.

Tossing the shovel to the side, he got down on his knees and began to scrape at the rocks with his fingers, dislodging them and tossing them to one side. He worked as fast as the packed-in stones would allow him.

It wasn't until he worked his way past a rather large rock that he realized something, the rocks should still be loose and not locked into the earth like this.

Panic gripped him as his hands worked around the large stone as he tried to pry it up. As he moved, a chip of the stone sliced into his fingertips but he did not flinch.

A few drops of his blood mixed with the soil and packed into the open cuts, sealing the wounds almost immediately.

In an act of anxious rage, he jammed his hands as deep under the stone as they would go and pulled upward as hard as he could, feeling the muscles in his shoulders and back strain. A broad slab of stone tore loose from the ground and sent him reeling backward as he dropped it back down.

As he sat on the ground, inspecting his gnarled hands, he came to the conclusion that he was in the wrong spot. He would have remembered such a stone when he was digging before and would have moved around it.

He also did not remember putting a heavy slab like that back into the ground. The answer was simple enough. Allen had dug in the wrong place.

He shifted his head to the left and then the right. The place looked familiar enough, evergreen trees with heavy, low hanging bows full of needles, a forest floor full of dark brown mountain soil, burnt orange and yellow needles, and small rocks here and there.

The same exact place he had just spent his morning. The same exact place where he had buried the body of a woman whose open, lifeless eyes had burned a hole into his soul.

*   *   *

A few hours before then and a short distance from the truck, Allen adjusted the heavy tarpaulin resting on his back as he walked up the narrow path to begin his morbid task. He hadn't been up this trail since he was a kid hunting with his father but it felt familiar in spite of the time that had passed.

He thought that maybe his mind was searching for something recognizable to ground itself due to the current situation. He was calm and steady so he did not dwell on the subject for too long before moving further up the mountain.

While the trail wasn't dangerous by any means, it did twist and wind up a mountainside full of sharp rocks, notorious for tearing apart the boots of many Appalachian trail hikers with their hearts set on making the trip from Georgia to Maine.

Luckily for Allen, this part of the trail was closed until springtime. If it were any other season besides winter, he would have had a slew of hikers, campers, and outdoorsmen to worry about.

He trudged up the slope, a few miles from the peak of the mountain, sweating hard against the cold nip in the air. His tarped pack wasn't very heavy but it also wasn't light. It was somewhere in between the two and just enough to be annoying on his back and shoulders.

Allen had worked construction for many years so a load this size was more than manageable, even on a steep mountain trail despite the aches and groans his muscles were making. He continued his walk up the mountain where he would bury the woman.

*   *   *

A while later, as the sun fell below the crest of the mountain, his muscles screamed in agony as he began to quickly dig in yet another location. There were a dozen small holes scattered throughout the ravine, varying in size and depth.

His strategy had evolved over the course of digging and now he only dug until he hit rock then he would get down on the forest floor and start to pull out the stone. If it was tight and packed down with dirt, it meant that he was not in the right location.

The more holes he dug, the more he questioned his thought process. He had no idea what the differences were between a rock packed into the dirt and a rock that was recently buried. He was only guessing to save himself some time.

Now he realized that his guess was wrong. He stopped digging and inspected his surroundings. All of the trees looked the same and to make matters worse, there were small holes dug throughout them.

Then it hit him, maybe she wasn't there at all. He stared at his blood and dirt matted hands while he theorized about his situation. Stress from everyday life or a midlife crisis had led to a fractured mind, a nervous breakdown.

Wondering if there was a tarp wrapped body at all, he stood up so that he could get to his cell phone. He checked it and found that all of the communications from his mysterious employers were gone.

With that information, Allen decided that he was out of his mind. The entire situation had unfolded in his own head. He never went to a random house in suburbia to pick up the dead body of a woman folded into a blue plastic tarp.

He had spent the morning digging holes on a mountainside to bury an imaginary body.

For some reason, his mind took him to the location that held some significance as a childhood memory. Memories of his long-dead father. A man who had suffered from memory loss in his old age.

"That's it," Allen mumbled to himself.

It was genetic and the Alzheimer's that had caused his father to become confused toward the end of his life had now been handed down to him. He dwelled on these truths for a while and he finally had himself convinced. It had all been in his head.

Allen looked around at all of the holes and chuckled to himself. Despite the fact that he was losing his mind, he was elated at the realization that his horrible task had never existed in the first place. He laughed heavily and heartily, filling the forest with the sound.

Wiping tears of laughter from his eyes, he slung the shovel over his shoulder and took a few steps in the direction of the trail. That was when he saw it. The place where he had vomited after seeing her face.

His eyes glanced at the spot and moved imaginary steps from its location to where he had buried her. It was empty of holes but the leaves and brush seemed slightly disturbed where he had swept it with the pine bow. Sweat began to form on his cold brow as he stared in horror at the forest floor. Maybe it was real after all.

Pushing his thoughts back down, Allen began to dig again. He couldn't tell if the soil was easier than the last few places but once the shovel clanged against a rock, he knew it was the right spot.

Unlike the previous pits, these rocks were placed in a layer underneath the dirt and it was so loosely packed around them that he easily plucked a half dozen or so out of the ground with ease, exposing the faint blue color of the tarp.

It was too late now. He needed to get it done and he needed to do it fast. The sun was well below the crest of the mountain, casting ominous shadows among the trees, signaling the coming of night.

While his mind was screaming, his actions were calm as he carefully folded the tarp away from her face to expose her mottled gray skin.

This time, he was ready for her open foggy eyes. What he was not ready for was her crooked, smashed nose. Allen thought he was careful when he placed the rocks but he was not careful enough.

One of the heavy stones had crushed her face, bending the tip of her nose almost to her cheek and splitting the skin along the line where the nostril met the upper lip.

There was no blood from the dead woman but Allen thought he could see the small black pit of the skull's nose cavity where her nose had torn away from the flesh.

He grimaced audibly and turned his head away in disgust. Stifling another bout of vomit, he tried to focus on the setting sun and the fact that his employers were expecting this picture.

Reaching into his back pocket, he pulled out his phone and thumbed to the camera app. This time, he made sure that her face was in the picture as he pressed the button to take the picture.

An alert popped up on the screen.

Battery too low to use flash.

He fingered the button again.

Battery too low to use flash.

The thought came to him, it isn't dark yet, I don't need the flash. Using both hands now, he thumbed through the settings and found the place to change the flash.

He turned it off and pressed the camera button again. There was no error message this time but instead, the screen went black. The phone was dead.

Half losing his sense, he raised his arm back to throw the phone but quickly decided against it. How would he take a picture with a broken phone?

He stood up fast enough to make his head swirl and before he could fully plan his next move, he was making his way back to the trail at just below a sprinter's pace.

Allen was back on the trail and still picking up speed. Stumbling over a root that was sticking out of the trail floor, he caught himself but maintained his speed once he regained his balance.

He was already more than halfway to the parking area. Once he got back to the truck, he would plug in his phone and get enough charge to take a picture. Then he would head back up the mountain again.

The sun was just starting to touch the tops of the trees, urging Allen to keep up his momentum. He knew that he would end up traversing the mountain at night, his main concern was making sure that his employer knew he was still on task and willing to complete the job. There was no doubt that they were aware of his phone being turned off.

Standing on the passenger side of the truck, he dug through the glove box, sending insurance cards, napkins, and a flashlight to the floor in the process.

Pulling out a charging cable and a cigarette lighter adapter, Allen connected the device to the truck with trembling hands and watched as the screen lit up with a red circle that read *1% Charging*.

Relieved that this leg of the plan was complete, he collected all of the items from the floor and put them back into the glove box except for the small flashlight. He closed the glove box with a slam and clicked the button on the back of the light a few times.

The clear glass lense blinked on and off as he clicked, bringing fresh hope to Allen and his scattered mind. He slipped the flashlight into his pocket.

He turned and moved to the other side of the truck, climbing into the driver's side of the cab. Checking the phone again, he saw that the charge was up to two percent now.

He had already decided that twenty percent was the magic number, plenty of battery life to get him back up the mountain to take a picture with flash and then get down far enough to get a strong enough signal to send a picture to them.

Watching the burnt orange light from the remainder of the day reflect off of the trees, Allen replayed the next few moments in his head.

Charge the phone to twenty percent, hike back up, take the picture, hike back down, send the picture, and put this whole situation behind him. He replayed the plan over and over in his head while he waited for the phone to charge.

*   *   *

Allen woke to the sound of knocking on the truck window. For a moment, he forgot where he was until a second knock on the glass shook the sleepiness from his thoughts.

He looked out of the windshield of the truck and saw the forest bathed in the red glow of sunset. It wasn't until he turned his head to face the knocking that he realized that the sun had long since set.

"Officer Williams, State Police," the man outside the window identified himself. "Could you roll down your window for me sir?"

"I um," Allen mumbled as he reached for the handle to roll the window down. "Sorry officer... I..."

"Sir, have you had anything to drink tonight?" the police officer interrupted.

"No... I just dozed off. I haven't been drinking," he told the policeman as he finished rolling down the window.

The cool night air rushed into the cab of the truck and sent a chill down Allen's spine as the red lights from the police cruiser lit up the trees like a fire.

As Officer Williams peered into the car with his long flashlight, Allen tried his best to put on his least menacing face. He didn't think it was illegal to sleep in your car and he had left the shovel in the ravine with the body. There was no outward sign of anything nefarious, just a tired man taking a nap in his truck.

"What are you doing out here?" Williams asked.

"I went for a walk to the top and back. Didn't realize how out of shape I was," Allen told the police officer with a slight chuckle, hoping that Williams couldn't hear the shake in his voice.

"The trail is closed for the winter. Those rocks can get slippery and dangerous. Didn't you see any of the signs?" the policeman said, motioning with his flashlight to the rectangular red sign posted immediately in front of the truck.

Allen shrunk back nervously, he did not see the signs when he pulled in or perhaps his predicament had caused him to ignore them. Either way, he doubted the police officer would believe that he had missed them.

"I didn't. I used to hunt up here with my dad and I don't remember the trail ever being closed," he told the policeman.

He was being honest. He could not recall a time when the trail was closed.

The officer did not focus on his lack of attention to the signage but had decided to hone in on the information about hunting instead.

"Sir, do you have any weapons in the vehicle? Shotgun? Rifle? Maybe even a knife?" Williams asked him, shifting the suspicion from drinking and driving to poaching.

"Oh... no, I don't hunt anymore. Not since my dad passed," Allen told the officer. "There aren't any weapons in the car."

He knew that the policeman was just doing his job but he also thought that the cop was grasping at straws trying to find something to write him a ticket for.

"What's in the back?" the cop inquired, his flashlight moving to the bed of the pickup.

Allen looked up into the rearview mirror and his breath caught in his throat. The blue tarp lay in the bed of the truck draped over the ovular shape of her body.

There was no explanation that Allen could grasp. He had buried the body on the mountainside wrapped in that tarp and he couldn't understand how he could be looking at it now in the back of his truck.

At this moment, he knew that his mind could not be trusted, moving back to the idea that he was sick and losing his mind. The thought also occurred to him that he had fallen asleep earlier than he had imagined and that all of the events leading up to this one had been a fevered dream.

Maybe he had never taken her out of the bed of the truck but fell asleep instead. Maybe there was now a police officer just a few feet from the dead body of a woman that he had meant to bury. The thoughts brought a fresh bout of horror to the already crumbling man.

"Sir, What's under the tarp?" Williams said, louder this time, moving the bright flashlight from the bed of the truck to Allen's face.

His face held a calm demeanor but Allen could see the undertone of concern in the man's face as he tried to diffuse the situation.

"Topsoil," Allen quipped. "My wife does a fair bit of gardening."

He felt the lie on his lips before he spoke it and in the short moment, after the words left him, Allen realized that he had made a terrible mistake.

"Gardening," Williams mused out loud. "Sir, it's the middle of winter."

The two men locked eyes for a moment. Allen could see that the policeman's eyes carried no kindness as he felt the tug of anticipation growing in his thoughts.

"I'm going to need you to step out of the car," the policeman said loudly as he stepped back from the door of the truck.

Allen watched as the officer's other hand reached to his belt.

"What? I'm just," He stammered.

"Sir! Step out of the vehicle with your hands up," the officer shouted.

There was no choice for Allen so he slowly moved his hands to the door, opened it with a loud creaking sound, and stepped onto the ground, his hands raised.

"Turn around. Place your hands on the truck."

Allen acquiesced. He knew that it was all over for him. Now, instead of having to explain a minute-long video of him cheating on his wife with a girl from work, he would have to explain how that video leads to him being caught with the dead body of a woman in the bed of his truck.

For a brief moment, Allen considered suicide. He knew that if he turned around and came at the policeman, he would be shot dead but he quickly pushed that out of his mind.

At least if he was alive, he could try to explain the situation to both the cops and his family rather than leaving everything a mystery.

Allen winced as Officer Williams pushed him against the truck and pulled his arms into the small of his back. He felt the cold metal of the handcuffs just before he heard them close around his wrists with a *snik*.

He did not try to resist or put up a fight, knowing that it would only make his situation worse. The policeman moved him away from the truck a few feet and forced him to sit on the ground in an Indian style position.

He watched the officer move to the back of the truck and pull up one corner of the blue tarp with one hand as the other moved the flashlight to look underneath the covering.

It wasn't long before he let the tarp fall back into place and Allen watched as he reached to the radio receiver near his shoulder and said something into it before returning.

"Sir, where is your wife," Williams asked him in a serious tone.

"She's away," Allen mumbled. "She's away on a work trip."

"Away on a trip," the officer repeated, staring fiercely into his eyes without blinking.

Before Williams could ask another question, Allen's phone chimed from inside of the truck. The policeman turned away from him and looked at the open door of the cab. When he turned back to look at Allen, the phone chimed again and this time, Williams paid his full attention to it.

"Don't move," he told him and walked toward the truck.

The officer found the phone plugged into the cigarette lighter adapter and Allen watched as his fingers flew back and forth on the touch screen.

Allen tried to think about the context of all the messages he had sent and received from the employers. He wondered if there was any damning information in them but he quickly stopped.

If the policeman had seen the body, he was screwed anyway. Williams walked back to where Allen was sitting on his legs, hands bound tightly behind his back. He held out his hand and showed Allen the screen of the phone.

"Care to explain this?" the police officer asked, thrusting the screen into Allen's face.

On the screen was a photo of the dead woman. Her dirt speckled eyes glared at him and the open cavity of her crooked, broken nose was rimmed with the yellowed bone of her skull.

As he looked into the hole, he imagined himself falling into it. Surrounded on all sides by walls of earth and scattered mountain stones passing him by as he fell deeper and deeper into a black pit.

Allen screamed. In his panic, he twisted in place, smacking his elbow into the window of the truck door. Fresh pain wafted into the remains of his dream and he slowly blinked his eyes open, revealing the dashboard of the truck and the vertical lines of leafless trees. It was dark outside, the sun had set and the white winter moon cast a silver light into the forest.

The panic from his nightmare mixed with the terror of reality. He had fallen asleep waiting for the phone to charge. The phone was still plugged into the dashboard.

He picked it up and held the power button in as he hopped out of the truck and jogged to the trailhead. There wasn't any time to waste and he prayed that it wasn't already too late.

He started at a jog but as the phone powered up, it chimed in his hand, he quickened his pace to a near sprint. No less than five messages had come through and all of them were from the employers.

We still have not received the picture.

Please confirm that the task is completed. We are becoming impatient.

We are currently unable to see your position. Growing concerned.

Please respond or the consequences will be severe.

And finally,

You have until nine o'clock. Then we will initiate our contingency.

Allen looked down at the phone as he ran. It was just before eight o'clock. He needed to move fast if there was any hope. Placing the phone in his jacket pocket, he produced the flashlight from earlier and turned it on, using it to illuminate the trail as he darted amongst the roots and rocks of the path as he ran.

Just before he had to turn from the trail and enter the pine gorge, his foot caught on something and sent him sprawling into the ground.

Sharp scraping pain slammed into both of his knees as they hit the mountain rocks but compared to what he felt on his arm, this was of little concern. A shockwave of jagged pain echoed from his elbow to the rest of his arm.

Despite the pain, Allen only lay on the ground for a moment before quickly jumping back up to his feet. He immediately checked his knees.

Blood was showing through his jeans but a few test steps forward showed him all that he needed to know, his legs were still functional. Picking up the flashlight that he had dropped during the fall, he began to run again.

As he ran, he carefully unzipped his jacket and pulled his arm from the sleeve. Just as he reached the area where he left the trail, he used the flashlight to inspect his arm. Much to his dismay, his arm was far worse than his knees.

Blood dripped in tiny rivulets down to his wrist and then onto the frozen ground. A jagged gash from his elbow twisted around to his forearm deep enough to expose the red flesh underneath.

His arm dripped thick blood onto the forest floor as he ran to the burial site. He wouldn't pass out or die from blood loss but it was enough that when he reached the hole strewn area of the body, he stopped to tear the sleeve from his jacket and wrap the wound.

As he bound his arm in the fabric, he thought about tracking a wounded deer with his father and following a trail of blood to the dead animal. The comparison to his current predicament resounded in his mind as he gritted his teeth and pulled the makeshift bandage tight.

Finding the vomit bush, he followed it to the pit. Her open eyes stared unblinking into the moonlit sky. Her jagged nose angled unnaturally to one side. Allen did not focus on either as he got down on his knees over her exposed face.

He had reached the point where he simply didn't care how gruesome or haunting it was. He had decided on his final push up the mountainside that the task needed to be completed now and that the memories of this terrible day would be sorted out later.

Reaching into his jacket pocket, his dirt and blood smeared hands found the phone exactly where he had put it. He pulled it out and without looking down, his fingers danced over the power button. The phone did not light up.

He pressed the power button again as he looked down at the device and what he saw crushed him entirely.

Irregular cracks spidered from one corner of the screen to the other. Frantically pressing the power and volume buttons with one hand, his other hand swiped repeatedly across the craggy screen, nipping his fingertips with the broken edges of the glass.

Thick tears of defeat cut clean lines through the dirt on his cheeks. Allen popped the back of the phone off, took the battery out, and replaced it immediately.

His face lit up with the glow from the screen as he thumbed the power button once again but his brief moment of hope was promptly dashed when the broken phone screen displayed only a solid white light.

The shattered screen showed nothing. There was no way for Allen to operate the phone.

His tears evolved into sobbing and without knowing what he was doing, Allen repeatedly lifted the phone as though he was taking the picture, even though the phone was incapable of doing so.

Allen sat like that until the winter cold bit into his fingers. Then without another thought or another tear, he stood and picked up the shovel. He worked to cover the woman's horrific dead face with soil and once again kicked leaves and branches over the location.

He briefly considered filling in all of the smaller holes that he dug but decided that there was no point. Once he made his way down the mountain, it was all over for him. He imagined Officer Williams and a flood of police cars filling the parking area.

Trudging down the mountain with the shovel over his shoulder, Allen was considering his options when he heard the phone chime again. He pulled it from his pocket and upon finding the still white screen, he laughed.

It was a deep belly laugh of a man that had nothing else to do but laugh. The forest was filled with his laughter as he made his way down the mountain path.

There were no police waiting in the parking area. There were also no police waiting for him at his house although he half expected to be tackled the moment he exited the truck.

Cautiously sliding his key into the lock of the front door, he opened it slowly, fully expecting someone to be waiting for him, either the police or the employers. Once in the house, he checked each room, carefully opening doors and turning on lights. The house was empty.

Finally convinced that he was alone, he sat down at his desk. Dirty, bloody, and stressed beyond his limits, he only thought of one thing he could do. He turned on his computer and waited for it to load.

Allen opened up his social media account and began to type out a goodbye message to his wife. He knew it wouldn't be enough to stem the tidal wave that was quickly approaching but it was the only thing he could do.

Allen hammered away on the keyboard, wincing against the pain in his arm from the fall. Even with the pain, he managed to consolidate his thoughts and explain everything that had transpired to his loving wife. He read it over and over again not fully believing the story written by his own hand.

A car stopped outside and Allen heard a set of car doors slam closed. Assuming it was the police, he clicked the send button and bolted to the front door.

Noone came to the door and after a while, Allen peered through the curtains to discover a silver sedan. He watched for a moment and saw a teenage boy leave his neighbor's porch. The boy carried a thermal bag like one of those delivery food services. His neighbors had ordered takeout.

When he returned to the computer, his screen had a new message notification on it. Instantly filled with dread, Allen opened the message, guessing that it was a response from his wife. It was not.

A deposit has been made in your bank account. The video of your indiscretion has been destroyed. Thank you for your compliance.

His mouth hung open as he read the screen over and over. Everything was fine. The police were not on their way and no one would be waiting in the darkness to eliminate him.

After a few moments, the message disappeared as well as the anonymous account that had sent it. Allen sat back in his chair, covered his tired face with his dirty hands, and wept.

Berks County. , PA. (WTOC) - The Berks County Sheriff's Office is leading an investigation after receiving a tip from a concerned citizen, ultimately leading them to discover a dead body.

The body has been identified as Susan Coulson, 26. According to Sheriff Alvin Knight, Coulson's body was found in a makeshift grave in a wooded area off of the Watershed Trail, a popular summer hiking destination.

Police have conducted multiple interviews and gained information that led to the execution of a search warrant at a home in the 200 block of the Conewago Valley housing development as well as in the Watershed Trail area. Cadaver dogs were on loan from the State Police but were ultimately not required.

"With the help of cellular data, we followed the suspect's movements to the area of the mountain where the body was found," a representative for the Sheriff told reporters. "The signal was partially lost but the suspect left a trail of blood from an open wound directly to the burial site."

Prosecutors claim to have a large amount of evidence in the case, including digital photos and data recovered from a broken cell phone but also said that a source close to the suspect had turned in a written confession to police prior to the investigation.

Allen Johnston, 49, has been charged with Felony Murder. Additional charges and arrests are pending as this is an active investigation. No motive for the crime has been determined.

<u>Smart</u>

The blaring alarm could be heard from one end of the dormitory hallway to the other. It rang for two minutes, automatically snoozing itself for five minutes before starting the process all over again.

Nearly an hour had passed with the cell phone alarm cycling over and over again until it was silenced by a hollow knock on the door.

"Yeah. I'm up. Sorry," a muffled voice mumbled through the door.

The door did not open but a shuffling could be heard within the room.

"Second time this week Andy," the door knocker told him "If it happens again, I'm going to have to notify the T.A."

Andy didn't bother responding. He knew he was in the wrong. Scooping a pile of clothing from the floor, he quickly sorted through it, holding each piece up to his face to smell it before either tossing it back onto the floor or his disheveled bed.

One pair of gray athletic pants, a red tee-shirt, and a black hooded sweatshirt sporting the C.V.C. logo remained on the bed.

Briefly considering the time, he decided not to risk getting a shower. He was already a few minutes behind schedule and he still needed to get dressed, collect his books and notes, and find something to eat before his class.

Andy was a sophomore at Central Valley College and he wasn't entirely sure that he would make it to his junior year. His freshman courses were difficult and this year was even more difficult.

College was challenging to say the least and Andy often regretted his decision to attend the more prestigious school instead of the community college near his home town.

While other students were having the time of their lives, Andy found himself hundreds of miles from home and struggling to maintain decent grades.

Collecting his scattered array of books, notes, and his laptop, he put them all into his backpack in a very disorganized manner. He grabbed a bottle of water from the mini-fridge next to his disaster of a desk and headed to the door of his dorm room, surprisingly only a few minutes behind schedule for his ten o'clock class.

The cafeteria was a short walk across campus but Andy did not have time to make it there before his class. He chose a pack of blueberry toaster pastries from the vending machine down the hall from his class as well as an iced coffee.

It was not the breakfast he wanted but it was the most convenient. If he was late again, he would be docked a few points, and his grades were already suffering.

Andy was far from dumb. In fact, he had gotten into Central Valley on a partial scholarship. His transcripts from high school were stellar and his grade point average was well over 3.0, earning him a position in the top ten percent of his graduating class.

Extracurricular activities included both sports via the track and field team as well as the more academic debate and chess clubs.

Having a good head on his shoulders, he had been prepared to apply for college. After much debate, he had decided on a degree in industrial engineering.

He pictured himself owning his own firm specializing in consulting businesses on manufacturing processes, procedures, and how to make their operations more efficient.

When he closed his eyes, he imagined standing in a boardroom with graphs, charts, and printouts, ending his pitch to the wide grins of corporate big wigs willing to shovel money his way to make their businesses more profitable.

"Mr. Baker," a voice interrupted. "If you must nap, please do it elsewhere."

Andy opened his eyes to see the instructor pointing towards the double doors leading out of the small lecture hall.

"Sorry sir, I…" he stammered.

"No, I'm sorry," the instructor interjected. "I really must insist."

His teacher motioned to the door with his arm. Andy slowly packed up his things under the scrutiny of his staring classmates and headed towards the door.

As the door closed behind him, he heard the lecturer mutter something and the class erupted in a roar of laughter. Letting out a heavy sigh, he trudged off in the direction of his next class even though it didn't start for another hour.

The next class was uneventful, mostly because he daydreamed his way through it. Andy had initially made an honest effort to pay attention but as the lecturer droned on he lost more and more focus.

He tried multiple times to refocus himself, including downing the iced coffee he had picked up earlier but it was no use. His lack of concentration was absolute.

By the time Andy returned to his dorm room during the two-hour gap in between classes, he felt exhausted. Despite the fact that he had gone to bed early the night before and had slept late, the only thing he could think about was sleep.

Setting an alarm to get up for his next class, he climbed into his disheveled bed without even taking off his clothes and promptly fell asleep.

When he woke up, it was dark outside. Reaching for his phone and thumbing the screen showed the time of eight thirty-four. He had slept through his alarm and both of his afternoon classes.

Andy let out a heavy sigh as he sat up. He felt drained in defiance of the many hour nap he had just taken. Rubbing his eyes, he stood and moved to the messy desk on the other side of the room.

Shuffling books and papers out of the way, Andy pulled his laptop out of the backpack and set it up on the open space he had just created, leaning back in the chair and stretching out his arms until hearing the chime that alerted him to the computer booting up.

He checked on his missed class to see if there were any assignments. Much to his dismay, there was a small research project but something he should be able to get done that night, especially considering his lack of productivity during the day.

Even though he had slept through the class, he found himself dodging the assignment and procrastinated by reading the news, browsing new threads on Reddit, and scrolling through his various social media accounts. Andy knew that he should be working on the project but he just could not bring himself to focus on the task at hand.

While browsing a message board, Andy noticed an advertisement in the corner of the screen. Normally, these did not appeal to him and were just a required nuisance of the internet but the ad seemed to describe his current mood exactly.

"Feeling burnout? Brain fog? Bad mood? Mental exhaustion? From poor diet to toxins in the air, the world around you is constantly diminishing the potential of your brainpower."

Andy's cursor hung over the advertisement for a long while, hesitant to click. Much to his surprise, the ad changed again as he waited to press the button.

"Nootropics or Smart Drugs are designed to nourish your mind with ingredients that immediately enhance focus, boost energy, mood, and creativity while supporting long term brain health."

He waited to see if the message would change again and sure enough, for a third and final time, the ad changed.

"Our specially engineered formula can help improve memory as well as increase your learning rate and cognitive performance. Your life's potential relies on your mind. Change your life today!"

With no more hesitation, Andy followed the link to the advertiser's website. It was a legitimate website, like hundreds he had seen before, that specialized in supplements. The page had everything from standard vitamins and minerals to weight-loss drugs and everything in between.

He found his way to the categories section, discovering the *smart drugs* category halfway down the list. Andy clicked on the link. Even before the page loaded, he had opened a new window in his browser and typed *nootropics* into the search bar.

For the next few hours, Andy scoured the internet on the subject of smart drugs. While not approved by the FDA, he found that the internet was filled with thousands of people who swore by the pills with a multitude of reviewers claiming the effects to be life-changing.

Andy read about dosages, side effects, and the best kind of nootropics to buy. At most, the side effects would make him sweat and lose his appetite which seemed like a decent enough trade-off for what everyone was claiming that they do.

Internet claims concluded that people taking the drugs were crushing it in their studies, their jobs, and even the stock market. More extravagant folks using the drugs were allegedly writing full novels in a day or composing musical scores that rivaled classics. The drugs provided energy, clearer thoughts, and improved focus, which was exactly what Andy was missing.

The pills were not illegal in the United States and could be ordered straight to his dorm; however, the hitch in the plan was the price. Nootropics, even the cheaper brands, were very expensive. Andy could not afford the smallest order of the apparently life-changing pills.

When he concluded that the miracle cure for his trouble could not be had, he crawled back into his bed. While only wanting to sleep, his body still had plenty of energy from the nap earlier and he could not fall asleep, even after lying in bed for almost an hour. It was during his tossing and turning in an attempt to find sleep that he found a solution to his problem.

Andy had been on the dark web a handful of times, being careful not to delve into the riskier areas of the hidden internet. Another student at the college had turned him onto it for the purpose of buying pot. While he wasn't a pothead per se, Andy dabbled here and there, mostly saving it for special occasions or after a heavy cramming session for one of his classes.

Access to the dark web had been limited to a black market site that sold drugs without the need for a prescription, illegal drugs, and bootleg brands of expensive drugs. He used it to buy pot because it was cheap and because they delivered it right to his door.

Before being introduced to the site, Andy had always been hesitant to buy it based on the locations he would have to go and the people he would have to meet. The alternative to meeting sketchy people in sketchy places was to buy it from one of his friends but more middlemen always meant higher prices.

Being careful to follow all of the steps to maintain his security, Andy fired up an incognito program before proceeding to open up the dark web browser. Moving through the appropriate pages, he found the link to the black market site and clicked it, producing a familiar screen promising cut-throat prices without the need for a prescription. He typed *nootropics* into the search bar and pressed the enter key.

Andy was happy to find a slew of smart drugs listed on the results page. Some of the names he recognized from his few hours of research on nootropics and other names he did not. Almost all of them showed generic capsules with no stamps or insignias with a matching all-white bottle void of labels.

Opening a normal browser window, he compared the prices of the name brand drugs on the clear net to the prices listed on the black market dark web page. He was not surprised at the significant cost savings and was elated for thinking about using the dark web to save himself some money.

Andy settled on a smart drug called "Red Focus" and found it amongst the listings on the dark web site. Scrolling down the page, he found the ingredients to make sure the lack of name brand didn't mean he was getting a placebo.

During his research, when he had settled on this particular smart drug, he had found that the primary ingredient in "Red Focus" was a plant from South America. The name of the plant was listed right on the top of the ingredients section of the black market page, *Sanguis Radix* or in English, blood root.

He didn't get too involved in the ingredients but he knew that a certain chemical found in the roots promoted healthy brain activity and stimulated his neural synapses. Without understanding exactly what that meant, he had reverted to a handful of user reviews on the clear net site as well as some YouTube videos on the wonder drug.

Whatever was in the ground-up root capsules made people think on their feet, made them focus, and increased their ability to learn. Given his current situation in school, this was exactly what Andy needed. As his father would say, "A good kick in the ass to jump-start things."

Andy added "Red Focus" to his shopping cart and went through the checkout process, making sure to use his bitcoin wallet to pay for the pills since it was more secure. Normally he would be paranoid about ordering drugs online but since this was merely a knock off of a brand name, he didn't worry much about the legality of it.

Managing to not get kicked out of any more classes, Andy plodded through the next few days of classes. As always, he did battle with alertness and lack of motivation with the usual arsenal of caffeine, too much sleep, and on certain occasions cold showers. These battles ended like they always do, zoning out in class, bombing pop quizzes, and slowly dipping grades.

When the package arrived at his dorm door a week later, Andy became paranoid, forgetting completely about ordering the smart drugs in the first place. Once he opened the box and found the unlabeled pill bottle carefully bubble wrapped inside, his mood changed dramatically. All at once, he found himself putting all of his faith into these little capsules.

The first time he took the drug, Andy made it more of a ritual than just taking a pill. Waiting until a Friday evening with no plans until Monday morning, he placed one of the red, powder-filled capsules on a white notecard in the center of his desk.

Next to the desk, he had stacked a case of water and on top of that, he had a case of Cup O' Noodles. He had no intention of leaving his room until he found out what these drugs did to him, constantly thinking of the warning on the website: "Results May Vary."

He sat at his desk for a long while staring at the pill, willing his hopes into the drug, hoping it would help him. Andy picked up the capsule delicately, placed it on his tongue, and swallowed it down with a mouthful of water. He felt it glide down his throat like a tiny prayer. Andy sat anxiously waiting for the wonder drug to kick in.

Eight hours later, Andy's room was in impeccable condition. Clean clothing lay folded in his dresser drawers and hung in the small closet. Dirty laundry was piled in the basket.

His bed was made. The floor, once littered with a random assortment of assignments, books, empty food containers, and clothing was not only clear of debris but had been vacuumed as well.

A trash bag sat by his door with cardboard boxes resting on either side, filled with recycling, sorted by types. The end table next to the single bed, frequently littered with half-empty drinks or snacks was clear except for a small lamp and a wind-up alarm clock.

The desk had met the same fate as the end table, cleared of refuse and adorned only with what belonged on a desk. His open laptop, a neatly stacked pile of books, and a pencil cup filled with assorted writing implements.

Andy was sitting at the desk with his headphones on, his head bobbing to music that only he could hear while the room echoed with sounds of keyboard clatter as he finished the last of his assignments.

Saturday morning, when the drugs started to wear down, Andy felt suddenly exhausted. It was no wonder, he had accomplished more in the past twelve hours than he had in weeks.

The nootropic wonder drugs had done exactly what had been predicted. His brain was firing on all cylinders and seemed capable of almost anything.

Beyond his immaculately clean and organized room, he had finished two lengthy class projects, had read a chapter ahead in his mechanical sciences class, and had even created an elaborate spreadsheet to budget his finances for the next six months.

The rest came hard and dreamless but when Andy woke, he felt refreshed and euphoric. Just one dose of the smart drug and He had never felt so good in his life. Andy glanced at his phone, it was still Saturday. Saturday morning in fact.

The sudden realization that he had only slept for a few hours made him think about how he felt even more. Despite the odd sleep cycle and the lack of time spent resting, he felt incredible. The smart drugs were going to change his life.

*   *   *

In the next few weeks, the wonder drugs fulfilled all of the promises made on the internet and more. Andy's grades were on an uphill trajectory and he was even working ahead of most of the classes that allowed him to do so.

In addition to his rising grades, Andy started to socialize more. He made a few friends since amplifying his life with the medicine, mostly because of his participation during class discussions. Without a second thought, he had even managed to tutor a fellow classmate who was having trouble.

"Andy, are you okay?" his pupil asked with a look of concern on their face. "You got quiet all of a sudden."

Andy looked at him with a pale, confused face.

"Yeah. I'm..." he said, stopping his reply as a fluttering feeling entered his head.

The feeling lasted for just a few seconds but it was unnerving. Andy had never experienced anything like it. It felt as though someone had poured seltzer water into his skull. The bubbling feeling between his brain and his bone didn't cause him any pain and only felt odd.

"Dude, if you're sick, we can do this another time," his friend told him. "I've got a final on Monday and I can't get sick."

His classmate packed his things up and said goodbye. Leaving Andy alone in his room to analyze the feeling in his head. He looked at himself on the camera on his phone, pinpointing the troubling sensation to his forehead. A long, dark vein lay under the skin and seemed very pronounced against his pale skin.

Deciding that he needed to get more sun, Andy moved his phone away but just before his face left the screen, the tingling began again. He moved the phone back just in time to see the vein in his forehead shift in its place.

Andy chose to focus on the analytical aspects of the sensations in his head. Thanks to the smart drugs, he always looked for the reason in things rather than reacting emotionally. Starting by entering his symptoms on a website, he thought back to the past few days and added headaches to the list. There wasn't a place to enter the information but he recalled missing time earlier in the week as well but decided it was nothing.

The diagnoses came up with a multitude of issues, none of which made any sense and varied from a mild case of dehydration to dreaded cancer and everything in between. Andy felt his head spin again and this time he focused on his forehead. He could actually feel something moving underneath his skin.

Pulling up YouTube, he did some searching and discovered a plethora of disturbing videos depicting people removing different kinds of larvae from underneath their skin. Botflies and hookworms were not uncommon, especially for people who spent their time outdoors. A light bulb went off in his head.

He had spent last Saturday hiking with some new friends. Dreadfully out of shape, he had spent most of the afternoon dragging behind the others but he was thankful when they reached the top of the lookout. The view was spectacular and he was happy that he had gone.

Just like in the videos he was watching, an insect of some kind must have landed on his head and without him realizing it, had put its larvae inside of him. The nootropics spurred his mind to approach the problem logically but a wave of panic also crashed in the background.

With the irregular mixture of logic and panic in his mind, he decided that he would remove the larvae from his forehead, just like the people in the videos. Most of them did it with a simple pocket knife and while the concept of having a bug under your skin was terrifying, Andy could not wait to see a doctor. He wanted this thing out.

Finding a box cutter amongst his things, he sat and watched a few more videos to prepare. It was no big deal, he told himself. Dozens of people on the internet have done it. When his mind was at ease, he walked down the hall to the dormitory bathroom.

Andy moved his face uncomfortably close to the bathroom mirror and reached up with his hand, spreading the skin on his forehead tight. He saw the dark vein underneath the membrane.

As he moved his other hand, the one clutching the box cutter, he felt the thing move. He watched in the mirror as it wriggled beneath his skin. Just like before, he could feel the movement in his head.

Its dance became more pronounced as the knife moved closer to his forehead. As it drew near, he moved his fingers into a v shape, containing the squirming vein. Andy drew in a sharp breath and slid the blade across his skin.

He felt the warmth of blood before he felt the pain. Andy knew that razor blades were sharp but he had expected more agony than this. It was slightly more than an annoyance.

Placing the knife in the sink, he ratcheted the dispenser next to it and tore off a length of paper towel. Folding it into a small strip, he held it in a line across his eyebrows to stop the dripping blood from getting into his eyes.

Looking into the mirror, all he could see was blood. Andy could no longer see the vein writhing under his skin. It was still and the bathroom became eerily quiet except for the *pat pat pat* of the blood from his forehead dripping into the sink.

Staring at himself in the mirror for what seemed like ages, Andy felt as though he was in an old western movie, waiting to see who would draw their weapon.

It drew on him first, pushing hard against the slit he had cut in his skin, tearing through the remaining membrane with a violent popping sound. Andy grabbed his head in both hands and hunched over in agony.

The pain was sharp and screaming as it spread the wound open like an animal trying to escape an enclosure.

He could no longer see himself in the bathroom mirror but Andy could feel the tendrils peel from the wound and dance against his hand, slapping them with wet noises that echoed against the smooth tile of the bathroom.

He felt sick to his stomach either from the pain in his head or from the horrific situation he found himself in. Prior to cutting open his own face, Andy had imagined cutting out a parasite like a worm or bot fly larvae.

Whatever kind of creature was currently residing in his head was nothing he had ever witnessed. Fighting waves of sharp pain, he stood up and faced himself in the mirror. Andy was shocked at his appearance, even before moving his hands away from his forehead.

Thick rivulets of blood ran down his face like a window in the rain and his dark hair was matted against his skull in heavy clumps. The white tee shirt he was wearing was soaked across the shoulders and hung heavy with the red liquid.

Andy's chest was pounded in anticipation. He sucked in a deep breath and moved his hands. A thin red tentacle flailed vigorously against his skin.

Andy let out a guttural scream and backed away from the mirror, fighting the urge to put his hands over it again. The tubular whip moved around his face, smacking his skin, tangling in his hair, and dancing in the air.

Without weighing any other options in his mind, Andy knew he had to get it out. Its movement alone was enough to send him into a panic.

"Get out!!!" he cried to himself in the mirror. "Get the fuck out!!!"

Andy charged back to the bathroom sink, picked up the box cutter in one hand, and grabbed the writhing tentacle in the other. It twisted and squirmed in his grip but he held on tightly, pulling it further out of the gash on his head. As he stretched the gruesome appendage out, he felt a jagged tearing pain from the wound travel down his cheek and into his neck.

The creature was long and judging from the pain he had felt, it ran from his head all the way to the base of his neck by the collar bone. Bracing himself against the pain, he pulled again, sending a fresh wave of hot, ripping agony. The tube pulled out a few more inches, spasming against his hand the entire time.

Andy tried a third time but the creature that spidered its way through his face and neck did not budge. Holding the squirming monster firmly, he quickly decided that before he lost his grip on the tentacle, he'd cut it off.

He thought that maybe that would kill the creature. He thought that maybe the rest could be removed later, in a hospital, by a doctor. Right now, he had to cut this thing out of his face, just for the sake of his own sanity.

Holding the writhing creature in one firm hand, he reached up shaking with the other, knife in hand. For a moment, he worried about cutting against his own head until he remembered that he was wounded already. The priority now was to cut the thing off, then he could stop the bleeding and go to a hospital.

As he began to cut, the tentacles in his face and neck held on firmly. The pain he felt indicated that the creature had extended hooks or barbs along itself. They dug into his flesh with the full realization that he was trying to remove it. Andy knew that this meant it was at least partially sentient, a thought that brought about a fresh wave of terror.

He had thought it was a vein and so, it would be easily cut through but he had barely punctured the skin of the tentacle. It was thick and fibrous, more like a plant root than a capillary.

"Sanguis…...radix," he sputtered as he cut.

"Blood ……..Roooooot", Andy croaked, stretching out the last word as he felt a wave of fresh, tearing pain.

Moving the box cutter in a sawing motion, he pushed harder and harder against the wriggling monster, digging the knife deeper into its sinew with each drag of the blade.

Without warning, his hand suddenly locked up, dropping the knife with a clatter into the sink below. All of the strength he was using had sent his hand into a muscle spasm and he shook it in front of the mirror.

Andy flexed his fingers and rotated his wrist to try and work the contracting muscles back into compliance but the more he moved, the tighter they became.

He stopped moving his hand and wrist with the hope that the lack of movement would stop the spasm. Catching his reflection, he paused for a moment to look at himself. The man in the bathroom mirror looked like the lone survivor of a slasher film.

The blood drained slowly down his face now, and thick clumps of congealed ichor formed in the crevices along his nose and mouth. His tee-shirt was ruined, completely soaked in the red liquid. Andy didn't care about any of it. He just wanted this monster out of his head.

The cramp in his hand was still present but he decided that it was well enough to continue. Grabbing the knife from the blood-spattered sink, he pulled it up to his head to begin cutting again.

Just as the blade fell into a groove cut into the tentacle from his initial attempt to remove the creature, his hand locked up again. This time he managed to hold onto the knife but pain welled up from the stiff muscles in his hands as he held on.

With a defiant groan, Andy forced the knife against the vein and began to cut. As he did, he felt the barbs of the creature dig into the meat of his neck again, holding steadfast against his attack.

While he cut, the sensation in his hand subsided completely but it was not because the muscle spasm had subsided. Andy could no longer feel his hand or forearm.

With a terrible ripping sound, thin brown vines erupted from the tips of his fingers. They pushed from underneath his stained fingernails, flipping them open like cellar doors. The large nail on his thumb tore off completely, falling into the ichorous sink with a tiny *clink* sound.

The vines wound out from under the nails, bent backward, and wrapped themselves tightly around his fingers before continuing down his hand and wrist. Andy was wide-eyed and screaming.

He let go of the tentacle protruding from his forehead and reached down to pull at the vines that were crawling up his arm. Except that the only thing he managed to do was to let go of the squirming monster on his forehead and put his hand down by his side. The vines had total control of both his limbs.

Andrew Baker, age 20, a sophomore in the Industrial Engineering program at Central Valley College watched in the mirror of the small dormitory bathroom, as he committed suicide by slitting his own throat.

The last thing he saw before he collapsed onto the floor was a tremendous stream of dark blood pouring from his open neck in a cascade of violence.

The vast quantity of blood pouring from the boy spread in a pool around him, running down into a small floor drain next to his body like the sound of water.

Without warning, the lifeless body arched violently, breaking his spine in the process with a sharp *SNAP* that echoed on the bathroom walls.

As the body slowly unfolded itself back into a more natural position, a thick wet slapping sound could be heard against the slimy tile floor as the mass of vines pulled themselves out of his body and slid down the drain with the torrent of blood.

Tales from the Dark Web

Tales from the Dark Web

Gambler

Donald Glosser walked through the high school cafeteria's double doors. He had graduated from high school many years before this moment and from a different school entirely, education was not on the agenda this evening.

Tonight's festivities included drinking strong black coffee, sitting in a dimly lit circle of foldable metal chairs, and the sharing of sins and everyone in this circle shared the same sin, an addiction to gambling.

Initially skeptical of the idea, Donald had finally decided to attend his first gamblers anonymous meeting but only after his girlfriend had packed a bag and left for her mothers for a "few days".

He knew that Sheila would be back but he also knew that if he attended this meeting there was ammunition that he could use to defend himself upon her return, not that he meant to use it. Like most men, he cared for his girl and he was upset that she had left, even just for a few days.

Unfortunately for him, the circle of chairs was by design so that no one could sit in the back and hide. In addition to the lack of hiding space, the circle also meant that the ball was passed to each person around it.

This was no figure of speech, there was a red rubber kickball, probably borrowed from the gymnasium across the hallway, that was passed from person to person to signify that it was their time to share.

Don did not like sharing. He wasn't anti-social but despite his girl's complaints, he did not believe he had a gambling problem. As the ball made its way around the circle and stories of underground casinos, dogfighting, debt, and losing fortunes were told, Don's belief only solidified in his mind.

He had never visited any shady card games or played back-alley dice. The closest thing to a dog fight he had experienced was betting on horse racing during derby season and the most amount of money he had ever lost at one time was barely a thousand dollars.

The only debt he had was some student loans and a bit of credit card debt but nothing beyond the average. He shared a nice two-bedroom apartment with Sheila and he always paid the rent on time. Donald had no horror story to share.

To make matters worse, the leader of the group, a colorfully dressed older man, was exceptionally talkative and carried himself like a professional. Whether he was an actual doctor or not remained to be seen and if he was, Don guessed that he was a therapist of some sort.

Embarrassed at his lack of plight and fearful of engaging the overzealous director, when the ball moved to his hands he attempted to hand it straight to the next person.

"I'll pass," he mumbled, hoping that the group's leader wouldn't have an issue.

The man next to him refused even before the director took notice and spoke up.

"My apologies," the colorfully dressed leader told Donald. "First-time attendees must share. Group rules."

Don stuttered for a talking point. He hadn't prepared well enough in his head because he assumed that he would be able to pass the ball.

"I'm Don," he mimicked the others before him. "My girlfriend thinks I'm addicted to online poker."

"Hi Don," the group murmured back with the group leader chiming in just after.

"Admitting that you have a problem is part of the healing process."

Don couldn't believe his gaffe. Blaming his girlfriend for his attendance was not the best way to avoid attention. The flamboyant man continued as if he were using cue cards.

"If you can't admit that you have a problem, then how are we going to come up with a solution? Studies show….."

As the older man turned from him to share this socially repetitive epiphany with the rest of the circle, rambling on about case studies and faith and strength for the remainder of the meeting. Don took advantage of the lecture and passed the ball to the next person in line.

"Sorry bro," whispered the long-haired guy next to him.

"I don't know you well enough to have taken that burden from you."

The man ended the sentence with a soft chuckle. Clearly he had been to enough of these meetings to know that first-timers had to share.

"I'm Charlie but my friends call me Chuck," the veteran whispered again. "Nice to meet you."

"I'm Don," he replied, understanding the absurdity in his reply as soon as Chuck bared his teeth in a humored grin.

"Yeah man, I know," Chuck laughed. "Everybody knows."

A week went by without Donald giving the gamblers anonymous meeting a second thought. He went about his usual routines, including playing a few hours of online poker, usually in the evenings after work.

Sheila hadn't returned home yet but when she had called him on the phone and he told her about the meeting, she had broken down in tears.

Don mentioned that he would be attending another one in just a few days as a way of baiting her to return home. She did not take the bait but she told him that she loved him and that everything was going to get back to normal both of which made him feel happy.

At the next meeting, Donald felt more relaxed. He knew where the coffee pot and donuts were lined up and he fell into the circle in the same place as last week, spying familiar faces around the row of chairs.

He sat next to Charlie who greeted him kindly.

"Welcome back," he told Don with a cheerful grin. "It's Don, right?"

"Good memory," he replied, matching the grin with his own. "And you're Charlie."

"Nah," the man next to him said nonchalantly. "We're friends now, so you can just call me Chuck."

Chuck added a handshake to the statement of friendship that went beyond politeness and entered the realm of personal. The arm that wasn't busy shaking Don's hand wrapped around his shoulder to give him a chummy pat on the back.

They spent the meeting whispering back and forth, killing the mundane words of advice and horror stories with bits of humorous anecdotes. Most of them were at the expense of the speakers but some involved Charlie's personal stories about how he ended up in the circle.

Each man skipped their turn with the gymnasium kickball. Since it was Donald's second meeting, he was no longer obligated to share. Chuck followed suit, flashing a grin his new friends' way in a show of solidarity. Neither of them thought that they belonged in the meeting.

The friendship felt natural enough but when the meeting leader noticed the chatter during the meeting, he took the liberty of assigning Don and Charlie to be each other's sponsors. Someone to call during a time of need when the urge to gamble was too strong for them to deal with on their own.

Neither man used each other to prevent their addictions from overtaking them as the program suggested. They did, however, take advantage of the exchange of contact information to meet up at a nearby diner. They continued to expand their friendship over the next few weeks, even visiting each other's apartments to share a few beers.

*　　*　　*

The moment Donald pulled onto Clay Street, he understood the seriousness of Chuck's situation. To call it a street was an overstatement and it could be more accurately described as an alley, despite the name of the road. It was the kind of single lane street that required oncoming cars to pull to the side to let people pass with either sidelined with the high walls of decrepit industrial buildings.

The narrow passage was made even more hazardous by the trash cans, dumpsters, wood pallets, and debris on the street. As he zigzagged his way through the obstacles, the light from his headlamps glistened off of every surface, as though the entire alleyway was perpetually wet despite the fact that it hadn't rained for days.

The GPS voice from his phone directed him to a tall brick building that seemed like it could have been an old warehouse. Large openings that previously held bay doors for shipping and receiving were boarded over with plywood stenciled with layers of graffiti.

A single yellow light hung over a gray steel door, clearly much newer and more sophisticated than the building itself. As Donald crept past the building, his GPS declared their arrival but he continued past the building to a small parking lot at the end of it.

A short time later, he stood facing the door, anxiously debating whether or not to continue. He didn't know Charlie very well, just a few weeks in fact and while he seemed like a pleasant guy, his stories about underground dogfighting lead Don to believe that he could have easily been an unpleasant guy as well. He tried to shake the thought from his head by focusing on the door in front of him.

The door itself removed any debate over the method of approach. Having no exterior handle, Donald's single option was to knock on it and see if anyone answered.

He rapped his knuckles against the gray surface and was surprised to hear a solid metal *thunk*, rather than a hollow *clang*. This door was solidly reinforced and meant to withstand a great deal of punishment before giving way.

Worried that the sturdy door had muffled his knock, Donald reached again to knock when a slot opened on the door at eye level. The person whose eyes appeared in the slot did not answer his knocks but merely stood on the other side watching him.

"Hi. I'm a friend of Chuck's," Don mumbled. "Uh, sorry. Charlie. I'm his sponsor."

Avoiding speech once again, the eyes behind the door cut him off by sliding the plate over the slot again. Donald stood and waited for a few moments before stepping back into the street. As he turned to walk away, an audible unlocking sound came from the steel door.

He turned back to it and watched as it started to creak open on heavy metal hinges. Don hurried inside, unsure of what lay ahead but feeling better knowing that he had made it inside and that Charlie was here.

Donald blinked repeatedly against the bright lights of the warehouse basement. In sharp contrast to the dimly lit alley and outside of the building, the interior was nothing short of luxury.

The interior walls were still brick but the dull red of the stone was painted over in a high gloss silver paint that reflected the decorative lights that hung every few feet from the ceiling. The paint and the lights effectively transformed the dungeonesqe basement into a bright and inviting atmosphere.

Dozens of well-dressed men and women sat, stood, or walked amongst games of chance, sipping cocktails and glasses of champagne. Blackjack and poker tables ran along the front of the space with a roulette and craps table dominating the center of the floor.

Against the far wall was a long bar that swarmed with the hustle of scantily clad waitresses collecting drinks for the patrons spread out among the games. Don was shocked that such a place existed outside of gangster films and television shows.

His shock must have been obvious because his escort, a massive bald-headed brute in a black suit nudged him toward a side door near the poker tables. Just like the doorman before him, the brute had also been mute. As Donald entered the side door, the scene changed again.

A neat yet unsophisticated office with a simple wooden desk position behind two wooden chairs greeted him as he entered. Charlie sat in one of the chairs. A portly gentleman in a garish red sport coat sat behind the desk, meeting Don's entrance with a smile that showed two gold teeth on either side of his grin.

Chuck did not greet him with a smile. He didn't even turn around or pick up his head and this irritated Don until he sat down in the chair alongside him and realized why.

Donald's anger was choked out at the sight of Charlie. One eye was nearly swollen shut and the other looked bloodshot and dazed. Splotches of dried blood clumped in and under his crooked nose and a deep crack split his lower lip in two. Charlie had been severely beaten and was barely hanging on to consciences.

"Your friend owes us a great deal of money," the man behind the desk told him.

"It didn't take very long for him to tell us about his gambling problem, how he was in a recovery program, and all about you."

Donald tried to speak but the man in red continued.

"He told us that you were assigned to look after him. He said that you would come here to help him and here you are."

"That's not exactly true," Don replied. "I'm Charlie's sponsor. I'm supposed to.."

"I know what a sponsor is," the portly man interrupted again as he reached into his breast pocket, producing a large coin and showing it to Don.

"Four years sober in May," he boasted while pointing a finger at the speechless brute. "Ray over there is my sponsor."

Ray remained silent, acknowledging the statement with a slight nod of his hairless head.

"Good. So you understand that.." Donald tried before being interrupted again.

"I understand that our mutual friend Charlie here owes me some money," the man in red stated, tucking the sobriety coin back into his pocket.

Don wondered if it was a coincidence that the coin was positioned over the man's heart. Perhaps he was more serious about it that Don had thought, despite his ignorance of Charlie's problem.

"I fully support recovery programs, I wouldn't be the man I am today without them but as a matter of principle, I do not mix feelings with business. Just to clear the air and make sure that you understand me completely. This is not a shakedown. I am not demanding that you give me any money or asking you to take on our friend's debt."

" I am simply making the statement that if you choose not to do either of those things, Charlie will not survive long enough to make it to another gambler's anonymous meeting."

As the man reached the end of his statement, Donald racked his brain with quick math to preemptively calculate how much he could afford to pay the man behind the desk.

As quickly as the thought came, another took its place. Even without knowing Charlie well and the knowledge that he had a gambling problem, he was still a human being.

Regardless of the debt, Don believed that all human life had value and he knew that he would help keep Charlie from being killed. He briefly considered the police but the moment he did, the man in red intruded once again.

"Before you consider your options, you should know that the police are NOT an option," the man said, seeming to read Donald's mind.

"The moment that Charles called you for help, we dug up everything we could on you Mr. Glosser. We know everything there is to know about you. Personal information, dating history."

"Hell, we even know your social security number and have your bank records," the fat man in red gloated with a sense of pride. "Isn't technology just grand?"

The man held his arms out wide stating the last line like a ringmaster introducing the next show, flooding the ears of Donald and Charlie with boisterous laughter.

*   *   *

The next afternoon, Donald and Charlie sat across from each other in their usual booth at the diner. They had not attended a meeting beforehand since there wasn't one scheduled.

This diner visit was meant to sort out the previous night's situation. They sat in silence for nearly an hour, ordering food and finishing their meals before Charlie finally spoke up.

"I'm really sorry," he started. "I didn't mean for you to get dragged into this. I'll pay them back and you won't have to worry about it. I've got something lined up that will fix all of this."

"Next thing you know you'll be telling me that it's a sure thing," Donald scoffed. He didn't mean to be rude but his tone begged to differ.

"Sounds like more bullshit to me. What are you wrapped into now? Dogfighting? Horse racing? Another underworld casino? What?"

"Look, I know that I haven't given you a reason to trust me after last night but I'm going to make this better," Charlie replied with tears in his eyes. The last part came out in chokes and sobs.

"My family and friends are long gone because of my gambling and you are the closest thing I've had since. I'm going to fix this. I need to fix this."

Don could only sigh and shake his head while his friend tried to reassure him. He did not see how bad the situation truly was and Donald was afraid that he wouldn't just inherit a debt to a mafioso but that Charlie would end up dead.

He didn't trust him to do the right thing but when Chuck broke down, Donald's humanity forced him to relax some. He changed the subject to more trivial matters to clear the air and eventually, their meeting ended exactly as it had begun, in total silence.

In the days leading up to the next Gambler's Anonymous meeting, Don tried in vain to reach Charlie. All of his calls went to a voice mailbox that was full and his texts were ignored. He didn't worry, Charlie had screwed up big time. He assumed that the embarrassment had finally set in and that Chuck was avoiding him.

As Don sat in the circle of chairs with the other gamblers, a heavy sinking feeling began to grow in his stomach. He fought the growing fear by focusing on the stories of the others around him but the tales of horrific gambling tragedies only made the feeling grow.

As his mind wandered, he daydreamed of the man in red and what he could be doing to his friend while he sat on the uncomfortable folding chair.

The moment the meeting was adjourned, Don made a beeline straight to Charlie's apartment. He made the drive in record time and when the elevator seemed to hesitate on the fifth floor, he jogged up the stairs to the third.

Without pausing to rest, Donald continued to jog down the hallway. His labored breath caught in his throat when he saw

Charlie's doorknob smashed from its place and dangling. Donald reminded himself to breathe and pushed open the door.

The small apartment lay in ruin. Furniture was flipped and torn open, cut open to be searched. The television lay smashed and broken in the corner. Smashed dinnerware littered the kitchen floor. Don walked carefully into the back bedroom to find it in the same condition.

Dresser drawer contents were dumped onto the floor haphazardly and the mattress was shoved against the wall, its springs showing through a massive slash in the fabric.

Donald instinctively reached into his pocket for his phone but froze as soon as his fingers touched it. The man in the red suit echoed in his mind.

"Isn't technology just grand," he remembered the man saying with his gold chipped smile.

Don felt the sudden urge to run. Every cell in his body begged him to leave the apartment. On his way back to the broken front door, that same feeling abruptly slammed on the brakes as his eyes locked onto the refrigerator.

Amongst the chaos of the apartment, the surface of the fridge remained clear except for a single, cream-colored business card stuck to the door with a simple magnet. Donald instinctively snatched the card from the fridge, slid it into his pocket, and continued his retreat from the ransacked apartment.

Later in the evening, Don woke up covered in a cold sweat. The excitement from the apartment had left him feeling drained and he had gone to sleep almost immediately once he returned home. It was the middle of the night now, just after midnight, and he lay awake still breathing heavily from the nightmare.

He dreamt of the man in red and his glinting teeth. He also dreamt about Chuck. The two were together again in the casino warehouse. Chuck was tied to a chair. The man was laughing excitedly. Chuck was screaming.

Donald tried to push the nightmare from his head, slipping out of bed and getting into the shower. As the hot water pounded against his skin, the calming effect of it helped to settle his mind long enough to remember the card he had pulled from the fridge in Chuck's apartment. With his mind racing, he hurried through his routine, wrapping up the shower and getting dressed in record time.

Finding his jeans on the pile where he left them, he pulled the cream-colored business card from the pocket and quickly realized that the text on the front of it wasn't in English.

From what he could tell, given the excessive use of the letter Y as well as the odd Slavic letters, Don guessed that the text was Russian. He sat down at his desk and flipped open his laptop, casting his bedroom in the blue hue of the screen.

In the glow of the computer, Donald pulled up a browser and began to punch the text into a translation website, carefully entering the odd symbols into the search bar.

Just before he pressed enter, he flipped the card over and revealed a handwritten web address stenciled onto the card in blue ink. It was a random series of letters and numbers with the stereotypical dot com at the end of it.

Don opened up a new tab, typed in the web address from the back of the card, and hesitated a moment to let out a deep sigh before hitting enter.

The website loaded into view, revealing an online poker site very similar to the one that brought him to this path. The only exception to this webpage and the one that he frequented, was that this page was in Russian.

Moving his cursor too and fro, Donald explored the site as best he could without it being translated. After a few minutes of probing, he let out another deep sigh and slouched down into his desk chair.

He wasn't sure what he had expected and while a large part of him remained racked with fear for Chuck, another part of him celebrated the fact that the website from the card was nothing more than an online poker hall. Tossing the card onto the desk, Donald stood up with the intent to return to bed, until something caught his eye.

The business card had landed on the keyboard of his laptop, just below the luminous screen. In the soft, gleam of the monitor, Donald could see the outline of a word on the card, imprinted onto it by something that was written over top of it. Snatching the card up, he held it close to the screen.

He squinted and could just make out the characters of yet another word in Russian. Without wasting time writing it down, Don entered the foreign word into the online gambling site's search bar without hesitation.

The moment his finger glanced off of the enter key, the screen of the laptop went black, casting the room into complete darkness. Donald felt around his keyboard for the power button to restart the computer but stopped short of pressing it when the screen flashed back to life in the form of a registration screen.

It felt strange that the page had suddenly translated to the English language while all of the previous ones had been in Russian but he ignored it, filling out the simple form in his native tongue.

The form did not require any personal data or revealing information. A simple username and password creation and an odd set of three graphics underneath. Donald was given the option of selecting one of three circles.

A red circle, blue circle, and a green circle. He instinctively selected the green circle due to the positive connotations that the color represented. Assuming that the graphic was a generic user icon that could be updated later to something more personal.

The moment he chose an icon, the screen morphed into a chatroom layout. Scrolling text messaging from other users ran along one side of the screen, with a large webcam stream on the other side.

Currently, the video showed a small circular lawn table surrounded by three plastic lawn chairs. Colored cloth placemats sat on the table at each chair. Each color correlated with the graphics from the previous screen, red, blue, and green.

The chatroom was quiet other than a few users greeting each other generically. Donald studied the stream intensely, wondering what it was that he had stumbled across.

In a few short moments, he would regret the money he had wasted over the years gambling online, including finding the business card stuck to Charlie's fridge and everything that had led him to this point.

Don's eyes refused to blink as the video feed showed three men being led to the cheap plastic table. Each man was undressed down to their underwear and handcuffed in the front. Even though they were each wearing a torn fabric blindfold and mouth gag, he recognized Charlie as one of the three.

As luck would have it, his friend was guided to the chair sitting by the green placemat. Donald froze in place while the chat log next to the stream exploded with activity.

As the other users filled the screen with communications, Don's eyes remained glued to the stream. They remained fixated even when the placemats were revealed to be burlap bags that were promptly shoved over the heads of the men, like medieval executioners hoods. Each of the hoods were crudely spray-painted with the color on the front, with Charlie's face being covered in green.

The shock of the video numbed Donald's mind to a point of apathy. It wasn't until the men were handed revolvers that he fully realized the full potential of the website he had discovered. As his brain struggled to catch up with what he was seeing, the men on the screen began to spin the cylinders of the weapons.

As the men fumbled to place the barrel of the guns against another's hooded head, Donald came to a realization. Charlie was playing an online game of Russian roulette to repay his debt to the man in red.

Donald tried desperately to close the browser window before the men pulled the trigger but a private message popped up instead.

"Isn't technology just grand," it read. He tried, again and again, to click the icon to close the frightening chat room but was met with another chilling message.

"Leaving so soon Mr. Glosser?" the message said. "The show is just getting started and we insist that you stay."

As he read the threatening message, the cursor moved itself away from the exit icon and back to the chat window, making the stream full screen. The instant the screen became bigger, a sharp *CRACK* erupted from the laptop's speakers, causing Donald to jump up and knock his desk chair backward.

The feed on the screen now showed Chuck in his green hood and the man in the blue hood sitting in their chairs. Both men held out the guns shakily, their shoulders heaving up and down with exasperated breaths.

The contestant in the red hood lay slumped on the bare concrete floor. The inside of his head weeping slowly down the wall behind him. From the positioning of the chairs, it was clear that Charlie was the player who had killed him.

The body of the dead man was dragged off-screen, leaving a sick trail behind it. Donald looked away from the gruesome scene, noticing with equal disgust that the chat was exploding as users professed their excitement or disdain over the results of the dual.

As they did, a screen flashed over the feed with the blue circle and the green circle. Without hesitation, Don selected the color that represented Chuck.

Unlike before, it was not a gut reaction based on the color of the selection, he was betting on Charlie, sincerely hoping that his friend would make it through this twisted gamble alive.

As the users made their choice, the revolvers were taken away from the still shaking hands of the contenders and replaced with freshly loaded ones.

The sound of the rotating cylinders alerted the gamblers to hurry their choice and as the men turned to face each other, Donald found himself gripping the edge of his desk painfully.

Chuck and the other man raised the guns blindly, feeling each barrel against the other's forehead. A voice echoed from the speakers and began to count down from three. At the count of one, both men pulled back on the trigger.

CLICK

Neither gun fired. Each of the men collapsed back into the chairs exhaustively as the hoods pulled against their gasping mouths, eager for fresh air.

Donald pulled himself away from the screen with an angry shriek, turning around and slamming his arms into his mattress over and over again until his rage subsided.

He lay against his bed for a short time. The metallic sound of the spinning revolver cylinders pulled him back to the desk.

Chuck and Blue had already found one another's foreheads. Both of their bodies glistened with sweat and each of them shook with tremors of fear and despair.

The voice cleared its throat before beginning the count again. One. Two. Donald turned his head away at the count of three but snapped it back to the screen quickly when he heard the gun fire.

Blue and Charlie both sat in the chairs holding the guns against each other. Neither man moved despite their nervous shaking from moments before. As Don watched carefully for something to happen, a thin wisp of smoke found its way out of the barrel of the gun held by the green contestant.

The player in the blue hood folded his arm to his side and collapsed through the cheap plastic lawn chair, shattering into many jagged pieces.

The man lay on the floor, the back of his still covered head to the camera, giving the gamblers a cadaverous view of the gaping hole in his head. A small glint of the grey concrete floor visible through the man's hollow skull.

Donald roared triumphantly as the chat came to life again with the conclusion of the game of chance, some riding high on their wave of luck, some dismayed at their misfortune.

With both his hands clenched into fists held high above him, Don paraded back and forth in front of his desk in a victory parade for his friend. A friend that he would be seeing again and not at recovery meetings. With the experience that they both had just endured, Don knew that neither of them would be gambling ever again.

Back in the stream, Chuck fell to his knees, letting the revolver fall to the floor in a clacking sound. His shoulders bounced up and down, sobbing uncontrollably. Having just murdered two people execution-style by shooting them in the head.

He could not understand how to feel but for the moment, the joy of being alive overwhelmed his guilt. Charlie was alive and he had repaid his debt to the man in red.

Donald was pulled from his celebration by noises from the laptop. Charlie was on his knees. It looks like he was crying. He knew that he could never understand what Chuck had just gone through but he was happy that his friend was alive.

Pulling the chair back up to the desk, he sat down, and turned his attention to the screen, anxious to see Charlie be released from the stifling hood and menacing shackles.

The man in the red suit appeared on screen with his back to the camera, producing a pistol from his waistband. Don watched as his friend's brain erupted from his skull, joining the spattering on the wall from the previous killing. ()

Large gobs of Charlie's brain matter rolled to the floor and joined those that had made the journey down the wall before it in a sick cascade of gore.

The man turned to face the camera, his wide smile showing off his gold-capped teeth just before the screen of the laptop went black. Donald screamed into the darkness.

<u>Delivery</u>

The red lights on the sedan flashed suddenly. There was nowhere for Zach to go. Despite the absence of traffic on the street, there was simply not enough room between the two cars for him to stop.

He pressed hard on the brake pedal but it was too late, the used, grey hatchback that he had saved an entire summer to buy slammed into the back of the sedan.

Zach's body was hit with a jolt but not nearly enough to injure him in any way. It couldn't even be classified as a car accident and could be better described as a fender bender. He was upset that it had happened but as soon as he unclipped the seatbelt and got out of his car, he began to worry.

The sedan in front of him was not an inexpensive car. Compared to his own, it was immaculate and clean, practically brand new. The only imperfection on its flawless exterior was a solid grey streak across the back bumper where Zach had hit it.

To make matters worse, the man who got out of it was dressed similarly to the car. A dark suit jacket with a blue shirt and a matching tie. To complete the ensemble, a tie clip and cufflinks shimmered in the dull orange lighting of the street lamps.

"Great," he thought. *"This guy is going to probably sue the crap out of me."*

As the man approached, Zach changed his mind about getting sued and quickly began to worry about getting beat up. In addition to the flashy accessories, the man sported diamond studs in his ears as well as a tattoo that stretched up his neck, stopping just under his chin.

"Hey, I'm sorry," Zach started. "I didn't think I was following too closely but you slammed on the brakes."

The tattooed man chuckled but said nothing. Unbuttoning his suit jacket, he reached into the inside breast pocket. Zach assumed that he was reaching for his wallet to trade insurance information so he turned around to go back into his car.

He shuffled in the glove box for a few seconds, finding his registration and insurance cards before climbing back out of the car. When he turned to face the man again, he was not holding insurance information.

The man from the expensive sedan was holding out a stack of money wrapped in a paper sleeve.

"I'll give you ten thousand dollars to drive off and forget this ever happened," he told Zach.

The man had a thick Slavic accent, possibly Russian, but it was soft and calm. The idea that the man may not have had a driver's license popped into Zach's head. If he didn't have a license then he probably didn't have insurance either.

Ten thousand dollars was a lot of money. It was well worth the superficial amount of damage done to his car. Zach did not accept the money right away and pretended to look at the front of his car while he debated whether or not to take the money.

He reconsidered the look of the man, the way he was dressed and the style of the car. It wasn't like him to stereotype someone but there was a high probability that this guy was a gangster of some sort.

Trying not to think about the dozens of mafia movies he had seen, Zach reached out to take the money.

If he didn't take the money, the guy would probably beat him up, or worse. Besides, ten thousand dollars was more than enough to not just fix his car but buy a new one entirely. He'd still have to keep working deliveries but it would make his life much easier.

As Zach gripped the stack of cash, the man pulled back on it slightly with a smirk.

"One more thing," the Russian told him. "I need the delivery."

As he spoke, the man tilted his head toward the back seat of the small hatchback. In the center of it lay a red, thermally lined delivery bag. Zach was confused.

"What?" he questioned the man. "It's just food. I work for.."

The man in the suit interrupted.

"You work for a delivery service," he said matter of factly. "We know."

Zach was shocked. How did this random stranger know that about him? Even more bizarre was the fact that the man knew that he was currently working and had a delivery order in his back seat. He started to get paranoid until he thought about what was in the bag.

The order had come from a pizza shop on the other side of the city. Randazzo's was a small, family-owned Italian food place that he frequently made deliveries for through an app on his phone.

He made plenty of deliveries ranging from fast food to fine dining and until now, this restaurant hadn't stuck out at all from the rest.

He would gas up the hatchback, grab his delivery bag, and log into the application. People who had a hankering for a particular food place that didn't deliver would place an order through the app. He would go to the cafe, diner, or restaurant, pick up the food and deliver it to their doors.

Depending on the size of the order and the kind of food they served, Zach made out fairly well, especially on weekends, rainy days, or anytime a big sporting event was on television.

This order was nothing out of the ordinary. A couple of sandwiches, an order of pasta, and a salad that were not anywhere close to being worth what the man in the sedan was offering him.

"Ten grand," he offered again. "For the bag in your back seat."

Stepping back and letting go of the money, he tried to process what the man was getting at. He couldn't understand why the guy wanted the food. Zach knew that the order was Italian food but did the guy know what the order was too?

In response to Zach backing off, the suit reached into his breast pocket again, replacing the stack of money that was in his hand. When he reached out again, he was pointing a pistol at Zach. His calm tone was also replaced, this time speaking forcefully.

"Give me the fucking bag," he shouted. "I'm not going to ask..."

The last line was cut short as the man gasped for breath. Dropping the pistol to the pavement, he reached up to his neck with both hands. They immediately turned red, covered in the blood pouring out of it.

His knees hit the pavement as he quickly bled out, turning his blue dress shirt an ugly shade of purple. His throat made terrible gurgling sounds and he slowly slumped over.

Without knowing what had happened, Zach just stood where he was, dumbfounded. The ring of his cell phone snapped him out of it. He pulled it from his pocket and answered the call.

"Hello?"

"Finish the delivery," the voice on the other end of the line told him.

"I got into an accident," he stammered. "I'm sorry it's late but..."

In his shock, Zach had assumed that the call was from the customer and in a way, he was right.

"We know. We can see you," they said. "Finish the delivery."

As they made the request again, Zach saw headlights coming down the street towards him. He walked out into the open lane and began to wave his arms back and forth, completely forgetting about the phone in his hands and the person who had called him.

A truck came into view but when it saw him on the road, it did not slow down. Instead, Zach heard the engine of the truck rev up and drive faster. Something was terribly wrong. He stopped waving his arms and remembered the phone.

"Hello?" he asked as he placed it against his ear. "There's a truck here but they..."

"Get down!" they yelled into the receiver.

Without thinking, he collapsed onto his stomach, scraping his legs in the process and looking up at the truck as it barreled towards him.

A loud popping sound erupted from in front of Zach and he watched as the front tires of the vehicle exploded. It lurched to one side, slamming into a street lamp, missing him by just a few feet.

The lamp crashed down on top of the truck, showering the bed in yellow sparks. Still laying face down on the pavement, Zach watched as the doors opened, and two suited men stepped out brandishing machine guns.

The moment their polished shoes hit the blacktop, their heads exploded in a cascade of violence. He did not hear a gunshot but Zach had seen enough movies to realize that whoever was protecting him was using a gun with a silencer.

Thinking about this, he put the phone up to his ear again.

"What the fuck is going on?" he cried into the phone.

"Make the delivery," the voice told him. "More are on the way."

The person on the other end of the line disconnected the call but he knew that they were still watching him.

Without understanding the situation at all, Zach focused on the warning. He needed to leave before more men with guns arrived. Pulling himself up from the road, he ran back to his car and saw the red delivery bag in the back seat.

"What the fuck is in that bag?" he wondered.

Climbing into the driver's seat of his little hatchback, he reached behind him. He picked it up, moving it to the passenger seat, but before he could unzip the closure, he heard another vehicle approaching the scene.

Without any hesitation or thought, Zach quickly reached into his pocket, pulled out the keys, and started his car. Backing it away from the sedan in haste, he heard a sickening crunch near his back wheels.

"Oh no," he told no one but the steering wheel. "Oh fuck!"

He had accidentally run over the body of the suited man but as more headlights appeared in the distance, he pushed the image from his mind and pressed his foot down hard on the gas.

Zach heard another wet crunch before his car lurched down the road.

The voice on the phone had told him to finish his delivery but Zach could only focus on the two trucks pulling up behind him. They were identical to the one that had tried to run him down in the street, dark gray with black tinted windows and a massive metal push bar mounted onto the front bumper.

The rate at which they caught up to him implied that the insides of the vehicles had been detailed as well. He could hear the roar of the engines behind him, picking up speed as they came closer and closer to his car that now seemed very small in comparison.

Coming to an intersection, Zach ignored the stop sign, blowing past it without care. His primary concern was the people trying to kill him and not getting a traffic ticket. He briefly wondered how a pair of flashing blue police lights would change the situation but the thought was cut short as the trucks cruised through the intersection as well.

With a loud crunch of metal and broken glass, a black S.U.V shot out of the side street and slammed into the side one of the chasing trucks, sending it spinning into a nearby building. Zach looked back into his mirror for long enough to see men jumping out of the utility vehicle and firing a multitude of weapons into the wrecked truck.

As he turned to focus on the road, an orange glow came through the rear windshield. The truck had exploded. An odd mixture of adrenaline, fear, and relief filled him and he glanced into his side mirrors at the remaining pickup behind him.

He felt the phone in his pocket begin to vibrate and out of habit, he pulled it out. It was a pre-programmed message from the delivery app. The application tracked the location of his phone at all times to let people know when their food would be delivered. It was letting him know that he was behind schedule.

In addition to the schedule reminder, his phone also reminded him that securing a five-star review for his profile was less likely if he made his deliveries later than the estimate.

"Fuck your five stars," Zach screamed at the phone as he glanced up at the rearview mirror.

A quick reflection of light came from the passenger window as it rolled down. Another suited man leaned out of it, aimed down the barrel of a machine gun, and opened fire.

He swerved back and forth, trying to emulate the racing video games he had played as a child. The back windshield of the hatchback exploded into thousands of tiny pieces and bullets ricocheted off of the metal frame of his car.

Zach hunched down as low as he could in the seat while still being able to see the road in front of him. The street was poorly lit with yellow lamps and devoid of other vehicles besides his own and the rampaging truck behind him.

The address suddenly came to mind. Zach hadn't thought of it before but the destination included on the delivery order wasn't in a typical location. It wasn't a housing development or an apartment building. The address was near the industrial area of the city by the ocean.

People sometimes referred to the area as the docks and it was packed full of shipping yards and warehouses. He didn't know why the address of the delivery didn't catch his eye before but he was happy that he didn't have to dodge pedestrians or other cars on the roadway in addition to avoiding the bullet spraying truck behind him.

As if on cue, his phone buzzed again, and he opened it to reveal a new message received on the application, it was a message from the customer.

"You aren't following the directions to the delivery location," the customer told him nonchalantly as though this was a regular delivery of food. *"Please get to the destination as soon as possible."*

The last part of the message read, *"We will take care of the rest."*

Zach looked up from his phone just in time to see the telephone pole.

Climbing from the open door of his destroyed car, Zach held his right arm with the left. Broken in the wreck, he could see bits of yellowed bone sticking through his torn skin. He assumed it was bleeding but between his blurred vision and the gashes on his face and body, everything seemed to be covered in blood.

His feet attempted to lift him from the driver's seat but dizziness in his head refused to allow him to keep balance. As soon as he tried to stand, Zach collapsed to the pavement. As he lay on the blacktop, he heard a car door close somewhere out of view.

Footsteps approached him and as they did, he realized who they belonged to, the driver of the truck that was chasing him. The person who was trying to kill him for whatever was in his delivery.

The sound came closer and Zach, focusing everything he could into moving, pulled himself on his stomach with his one good arm in a feeble attempt to escape. The footsteps stopped behind him and he heard the *snick* of a handgun hammer being pulled into place.

He rolled onto his back to face the aggressor and found a man nearly identical to the one he had rear-ended just a few minutes earlier. The man wore a black suit, white shirt, and a black-tie.

"Take it," he gasped. "Take whatever the fuck you want."

"That is no longer an option," the suit replied. "You know enough to be trouble."

"I don't know shit," Zach tried to explain. "You want my delivery. Just fucking take it!"

The man responded by lifting the gun up to aim. Zach watched as his fingers moved to pull the trigger. There was nothing he could do to get away. He closed his eyes and waited for the sound.

A deafening roar painfully erupted into his ears and he heard a scream but the voice was not his. He opened his eyes and saw the man in the suit pinned between the twisted wreck of his car and the black SUV that had helped him before.

The damaged door of the vehicle creaked open on bent hinges and a young man in a tracksuit jumped from the car, a pistol in hand.

Without checking on Zach, he calmly walked over to the screaming man pinned between the cars and ended his pain by pulling the trigger.

Zach clung onto consciousness, fading in and out of it as though he were blinking his eyes. He felt his body being lifted and placed into the SUV. He tried to talk but he couldn't be sure that the words came out.

Briefly fading into existence, he noticed his red thermal delivery bag on the seat beside him, before fading back out again.

The next thing he remembered was waking up to incredible burning pain in his injured arm. He opened his eyes to bright, searing light coming from above him. Zach turned his head to avoid it and saw an elderly man in a hospital gown lying on an operating table next to his own.

A clean looking, stainless steel table full of surgical tools sat next to the man and on a shelf underneath the table was his red delivery bag. Zach blinked his eyes to fight the sleepiness he felt in his head and watched as a doctor entered his view.

Just before fading out once more, he saw the doctor open up his delivery bag and pull out a small styrofoam container. It made a sloshing sound as he did, giving Zach the impression that it was full of ice.

The doctor carefully sliced the tape holding the cooler closed with a scalpel from the table and removed the lid.

"Intact and undamaged," the doctor exclaimed as Zach's vision went black. "And thanks to our friend here, we received it in plenty of time."

For the next few hours, Zach dreamt of strange things. He imagined that the doctor removed a human heart in a ziplock bag from the container he delivered.

Another doctor came to take the heart away, placing it on a clean metal tray next to the old man on the operating table.

A team of surgeons worked diligently under the bright overhead lights, stretching open the old man's chest with a popping sound that could only have been his bones.

An odd machine behind them pumped thick crimson blood through plastic tubes that entered the man's chest.

Fading in and out of reality, Zach saw the man's heart leaving his chest cavity in the blue gloved hands of a doctor and replaced with the one he had brought to them in his red bag.

The delivery that people had tried to bribe, threaten, and eventually kill for, was a human heart to replace that of the old man.

When he woke up, the old man was gone. The operating equipment remained but in place of the heart and the surgical tools lay Zach's red delivery bag and a single sheet of paper.

He rolled from the table, nursing his broken arm, finding that a thick plaster cast had been applied to it. He reached up to touch his cheek and found the gash sutured closed. The cuts on his arms were also bandaged.

Weakly standing, Zack carefully walked the few feet to the makeshift operating theatre. The walls on all four sides were simple plastic shower curtains and he could see walls on the other side of them. Looking up at the steel trusses overhead, he decided that he was in one of the abandoned warehouses of the docks.

The sheet of paper had few words written on it. A simple message of instructions to report his car stolen at the end of the week. He considered this for a moment and assumed that if these people he had unwittingly helped could pull off what they had last night, covering up a car chase, accident, and a multitude of murders was easily managed.

He turned his attention to the red delivery bag. Its handle was torn and it was covered in an odd pattern of burn marks and blood. He opened the zippered pouch.

Two pill containers rolled out of the mouth of the bag and out of habit, Zach moved quickly to catch them. His body screamed in agony as he moved. His cuts and arm had been mended but he was nowhere near being fully recovered from the insane night.

He was pleasantly surprised to see that the first bottle of pills were low-grade pain killers and even more so to find that the second bottle contained antibiotics.

Both bottles had legitimate labels with instructions and dosages. Whoever had left them meant for Zach to heal in relative comfort, probably so he wouldn't be tempted to see a doctor or go to a hospital.

Placing the containers onto the operating table, he turned his attention back to the bag. Unzipping the opening completely, he discovered that the delivery bag was full of crisp, neatly bundled hundred dollar bills.

According to the paper straps, each bundle contained ten thousand dollars, making the delivery bag worth over a hundred grand.

The money made him think about the delivery app. He patted around his pockets carefully nursing his stiff arms. Zach found his phone, pulled it out, and turned it on.

A notification from the app appeared in his taskbar and he thumbed it open. It informed him that his customer had left a five-star review on his delivery profile for a job well done.

Tales from the Dark Web

.

<u>Cure</u>

My trembling hand pressed harder against my ribs, bringing fresh invigorating pain. Brightly colored blood oozed between the gaps in my fingers and soaking my crisp white shirt making it stick to my skin like syrup. I just bought this shirt. It wasn't even on sale. No way that stain is coming out.

"Take it to mom," I startle myself with the sound of my own voice.

My mother swears she can get any stain out and it was damn near the truth. Why am I thinking of my mother and her lifelong battle with laundry in a situation like this?

"You're dying, idiot," I mutter nonchalantly.

The real problem here isn't the stain, I muse. The problem is the hole. Mom can sew but there would always be a seam where she stitched it up and that is enough to drive someone like me absolutely insane.

Yes, I conclude, the root of the issue is the hole in my shirt where, I would assume, a bullet entered. I don't know enough about the subject of firearms to continue down that path so let's just focus on what I know.

I purchased a wrinkle-resistant, white button-down shirt two weeks ago. It was not on sale. I paid full price and now the shirt is ruined due to a small hole just below the right breast pocket as well as a large dark red stain from the tear all the way to my belt.

I wondered if the receipt was still on my dresser but gave up that line of thought before concluding that I'd be dead in a few minutes and would never be able to return the shirt.

Footsteps crunched on the broken glass that was scattered on the floor and I squeezed my eyes shut, preparing for the end.

*   *   *

"Tuesdays are just Monday's ugly sister," I mumble to everyone and no one as I shuffle into the elevator.

A slight murmur and a shuffling of bodies greets me as they shamble to make room for one more dead-eyed, thirty-something desk jockey. I could make millions off of bottling the smells in this tiny space.

The stainless steel paneling that makes up the interior of every elevator on earth seemed to reflect the smells of the rancid sausage from a breakfast cart burrito and a heaping amount of Old Spice of the men. The overpriced coffee and knockoff designer handbags of the ladies. I'll bottle it and sell it to the masses.

"Smells of Dissatisfaction, The newest fragrance from Ryan."

"Excuse me?" My boss inquires, pulling me from the clouds of my daydream.

Damn. I must have said that out loud. The timing is terrible. I am in a disciplinary meeting.

"For someone with your experience and pay, we would like to see more effort going forward," projects the boss using his best motivational voice.

Much like his office decor, Mr. Bossman has a personality that contains an exquisite mix of encouraging self-help books and self-serving awards.

His current role as the office supervisor includes meandering about in search of employees to micromanage, regurgitating buzzwords and inspirational quotes from the many internet blogs he visits on company time.

The boss also spent time patrolling the restrooms to ensure that no single staff member takes any longer than a five-minute dump. I swear to god he can recognize people by their shoes. Note to self: start dress shoe collection for more conspicuous shits.

Tales from the Dark Web

I am a project manager for a small engineering firm specializing in You know what, it doesn't matter. What does matter is that I am bored out of my goddamn skull with monotonous labors like paperwork, conference calls, and client meetings. The most exciting part of my week is replying to the weekly email chain about where we are going for lunch on Friday.

I don't dislike my job. Believe it or not, I actually love my job at times. Every few weeks, I'll be handed a project that is challenging and those are the moments that make me love my line of work. The long, soul-sucking in between those times really kills it for me.

I find myself applying certain strategies to combat the black hole of boredom. Trips to the office supply room, idle chit chat, and frequent trips to the restroom all reside in my playbook. The above-mentioned dress shoe collection will be added just as soon as I can hit the mall.

Unfortunately, my battle with tediousness has recently been a losing one and I find myself coasting through even the challenging parts of my job. This has led to me dropping the ball on more than a few occasions. Sometimes it's a minor detail that doesn't take more than a few hours of scrambling to fix.

Other times its a cluster fuck of epic proportion, requiring wads of company cash to rectify. Each time something comes up, I tell myself it's the last one and for a short while, an effort is made to make it true but slowly, my dissatisfaction comes creeping back in to find the cracks in my spirit, like weeds growing in between sidewalk slabs.

The day after my meeting, I didn't go into work. I didn't feel sick or tired, it was more of an evolution of waking up late, realizing I had an abundance of sick time, and not wanting to deal with rushing around to make it to work on time. It wasn't until Friday, the third day in a row I had called off when I realized that something was wrong.

Staring into the mirror with bloodshot eyes and an unshaven face, it occurred to me that I hadn't changed clothes since I went to bed Tuesday night. That led to the thought that I hadn't left the house in three days and then to the fact that other than the automated voice on the call off line, I hadn't spoken to another human during that time either.

Something was most definitely wrong and much like my

internal struggle with boredom, I decided that everything was fine. Starting fresh the next week was my objective and every cell in my body intended to kick some ass first thing Monday morning.

Except that Monday morning came and went with me never having left my bedroom. I called off, of course, It wasn't as if I wanted to lose my job but at this point, I needed a doctor's excuse since our policies required one for absences longer than three days.

With that in mind, I called off on Tuesday because I didn't have the excuse. Then on Wednesday and again Thursday. Finally, on Friday, I managed to drag myself out of bed after making an appointment with my family doctor.

It was absolutely brutal. That sounds silly, I know, but it took every ounce of energy for me to just check in with the receptionist's desk. Every word spoken to me was like running my conscience through a windowpane.

Every thought fractured in my head like the webs on broken glass. The tendrils of a million questions and million answers all at once bouncing back and forth like the inside of my skull was a mirror.

All of that and all the poor woman asked me for was my insurance card.

The sight of me must have been alarming. I couldn't remember the last time I had showered or changed my clothes. I'd guess that my family doctor had me half diagnosed after just looking at me but after having a conversation about what had transpired in the past two weeks, it was confirmed.

No energy, thoughts of hopelessness, inability to focus, he concluded that I was depressed. I had officially become a headcase, complete with a script for crazy pills often seen advertised on late-night television.

Despite the medicine my family doctor had prescribed, the two weeks after starting on the antidepressants went exactly the same as the two weeks prior. Lots of sleeping, lots of lying in bed wishing I was sleeping, and very little in between.

The doctor had given me forms to send into work to take medical leave but even if he hadn't, I honestly didn't care if I ended up losing my job or not. Everything seemed gray and dull.

There was one thing that I did besides sleep those two weeks but it was the very opposite of being productive. Whenever I couldn't sleep, I would research suicides. Pulling information of all of the conventional methods, I spent many waking hours scratching them off my imaginary checklist one by one:

A gunshot to the head was too prone to failure, and I didn't want to spend 20 hours of a surgeon's time reconstructing my torn-apart face if I missed the mark.

Pills were a good option, but then again, my overactive imagination had me picturing the worst-case scenario. To me, that wasn't death, but an allergic reaction. I wanted my untimely demise to be peaceful and painless, not humiliating and riddled with hours of agony.

Bit by bit I rejected every other option I could think of: carbon monoxide poisoning through car exhaust fumes, slitting my wrists and even jumping off the tallest building I could find.

Looking back, I realize I was making excuses to avoid what I considered back then to be the elegant way out. Now I can see that just being a coward. I made a lot of excuses.

One afternoon while plotting my own demise, my phone rang. As it turns out, in addition to my family doctor prescribed antidepressants, he had given me a referral for a therapist.

The message on my phone explained that they hadn't heard from me and that if I did not call to schedule an appointment, they would send the police for a wellness check.

What I did not know at the time was that this doctor was not the one referred by my doctor and the threats of police wellness checks were empty. After my ordeal was over, I discovered that this particular therapist had utilized software to alert him whenever people were diagnosed with particular ailments close to his location.

The software itself was easily found in the shadier corners of the internet and in addition to it, my new doctor had also gained access to my personal records, social media accounts, and my entire background. All things he used to manipulate me into fulfilling his goals.

Without knowing all of these things, Dr. Lyle Abbott came highly recommended, seemingly just like every other doctor. He, however, boasted about his unorthodox methods from the very first session.

It should have been an ominous sign, but to me, it showed promise for a better tomorrow. If nothing else had worked, perhaps a different approach to my depression was the solution.

"No more medication," he told me right off the bat. "And no talking for hours and hours on end about feelings, anxieties, uncertainties. No ranting about how dull and boring your job is."

His solution to my problems, he explained, would be far more effective, and far less risk-free.

"You don't get to change your life by talking all day long about how much it sucks," Dr. Abbott explained, smoothly.

His tone of voice fascinated me from the start. It was buttery, warm, and enticing, without being overly complacent.

He was an elegant man in his late fifties, lean and well-dressed. He was the kind of bald man who doesn't attempt to hide the fact that his hair is long gone. No toupee, no comb-over, no cleverly-disguised wig. He was confident and smooth, yet there was something about him I always found slightly off.

Perhaps it was his eyes, blue and bright, always staring right at his patients. They were warm, yes, and even inviting most of the time, just like his smile. He tried to appear non-threatening and welcoming, but from time to time, I'd notice something else. Something lurking beneath the surface.

It happened when I looked away when I stared at the wall or at one of his diplomas instead of straight at him. On those moments, through the corner of my eye, I could see something shift in his gaze. Something predatory, almost obsessive-like.

In truth, he was both obsessive and a predator. Dr. Abbott had poured over my information and adjusted his methods according to his profile of me.

When I looked back at Dr. Abbott, though, it was long gone, and so I never truly gave my suspicions too much thought. At least not until the day I almost died thanks to his unconventional therapy methods.

I vividly remember the first time I met Dr. Abbott.

His office was, from the outside, another nondescript yet elegant building downtown. It was located in a nice area of the city, one you would walk through at night without looking over your shoulder.

I was surprised by this fact, considering his honoraries weren't out of my budget. Though I wasn't on a strained budget, I didn't have the income to regularly visit a high-end therapist.

I decided to take the stairs instead of going up on the elevator, already half-filled with two women who I could swear were secretaries, and three businessmen, or at least men dressed in fine enough suits. I spent too much of my day surrounded by their kind and wanted to avoid them altogether when I was off work.

Knocking on his door, I noticed myself fidgeting with my watch. I had secretly promised myself that if this didn't work, I would kill myself. For real this time, no more procrastination. At that moment, the selected method was sleeping pills and a bathtub filled with warm water, but I changed my mind so many times already, it was prone to shift again soon.

Much to my surprise, no pretty secretary answered the door: Dr. Abbott himself, dressed impeccably in a lilac shirt and black slacks -no tie-, was the one to answer and let me in. His smile made promises I was quick to believe in.

"You must be Mr. Brown," were the first words he said to me. I nodded. "Come in, please, I was expecting you."

"You can call me Dylan," I muttered sheepishly, as I stepped inside, looking around with interest.

He guided me through a large hallway, and into an ample, bright reception room. I was surprised not to see the typical chaise lounge immediately associated with therapy but instead large, comfortable-looking sofas facing one another.

The walls were almost completely covered with towering bookcases, except for the one featuring a grand window, through which I could enjoy a quick glimpse of the city.

"Do you prefer to be called Dylan?"

I was caught off-guard by his question and turned to face him. After a moment of hesitation, I shrugged.

"I don't mind either way."

"Then why make the clarification?" He asked, motioning for me to sit. I was baffled by the inquiry and mumbled a reply.

How could a person make you feel welcomed and anxious at the same time? Dr. Abbott had that quality, and he seemed to be quite keen on exploiting it to his advantage.

"I… well, I figured it was the polite thing to do."

"I see," he said, turning away from me to begin scribbling on his notepad.

Was he trying to make me feel anxious, inadequate, or was he simply taking down notes for real? I never quite got the answer to it, but he did it quite often, and for far longer than I believe he needed to actually write whatever it was he was noticing about me.

The first session was easy enough. I would have never imagined all that would come after it from that experience alone. He asked me questions about my life, my past, what brought me to him, and what my fears were. Why I was depressed, why I was bored, and what did I want to do about it.

"Have you ever heard about immersion therapy?" Dr. Abbott asked, close to the one-hour mark.

Our session was just about to end and only now had my curiosity truly been piqued.

"Immersion… no, I don't believe I have."

He rested his journal on his lap and leaned forward as if he was about to tell me a secret. I unconsciously leaned forward as well.

"It's usually a technique used to confront one's phobias or deal with anxiety disorders, but I believe it can be used for far more than just that. I believe it's the solution to your ailment, Dylan."

He spoke with such confidence, I suddenly felt like I was being offered a miracle solution, and much to my surprise, I wasn't skeptical about it.

"And what would it consist of?"

Dr. Abbott proceeded to explain to me his unconventional yet apparently highly successful methods. It would involve exposing me to increasingly dangerous and thrilling situations.

He told me it was a way for me to experience an increase in adrenaline and endorphin levels without having to resort to prescription drugs. He assured me I could be fully cured in a mere 3 months if I followed his program.

"I'm not certain I can afford it," I mumbled, trying to find an excuse to say no. Any excuse which didn't imply I was afraid and more than a little bit worried.

Doctor Abbott had already gained access to my financial records through his dark web programs. He knew that I could not afford a therapist. Using this knowledge, he tactfully laid a trap. A trap that I fell into without thinking twice.

"My fee is fully negotiable," he explained smoothly, granting me no space for arguing. "This is a new and novel technique, and I am quite interested in demonstrating it works. So you would be doing me a favor just as much as I would be doing you one."

I know he sensed I was hesitating, and he pulled out the big guns.

"It beats the alternative," he explained, almost nonchalantly.

"The alternative?" I asked, fidgeting quietly under his intense stare.

"Attempting suicide is a valid reason to keep you under observation for at least seventy two hours, and if your employers discover you've been committed to a mental hospital…"

At the time, I questioned whether or not the doctor was bluffing. Without my knowledge, he had already discovered my company's policies on the matter. They held an employ at-will policy. They could fire me at any time and for any reason. He had done his research.

"Are you threatening me?!" I exclaimed, utterly shocked.

His voice, his eyes were so warm, so welcoming. I never imagined a man like him could resort to such sordid methods. Though it did explain that odd feeling I got whenever I looked at him through the corner of my eyes.

"Not at all, Dylan. Think of it as giving you a little push in the right direction."

I hesitated but eventually agreed. I was oblivious to the obsessive nature of the man before me. He knew me before I had even walked into his office.

I became Dr. Abbott's guinea pig, without either of us genuinely acknowledging it out loud. I pretended I was an entirely willful patient. He seemed to honestly care about me getting better, improving my life and overcoming my depression. Just as long as I followed his every command.

It started innocently enough.

Dr. Abbott asked me to meet him at a nearby casino instead of at his office. We were about to engage in my first experience as a newfound thrill seeker. I felt anxious, entirely out of my element as we walked toward the high limit tables.

Men there wore expensive suits and wrapped their arms around gorgeous blondes with more breasts than brains. They sipped at their champagne flutes and threw the dice as if they were dealing with nickels and dimes instead of betting hundreds or thousands of dollars with each new roll. One man in a red suit and gold-capped teeth seemed especially menacing.

"This is too expensive for me," I mumbled, trying to find any excuse to return home.

The truth was, I just wanted to curl up on my bed until it was time to go to work, as I always did whenever my anxiety got the best of me. Disappearing from the world was what I did best, and I was too used to hiding to be comfortable in the spotlight.

"Come now, Dylan, it's not the time to try and find excuses," he told me. "It's time to take your first step, your first risk,"

Dr. Abbott coaxed me toward the table with his charming voice and soothing words. It felt as if I was slowly yet steadily approaching the edge of a cliff. I wanted to run away just as much as I wanted to obey.

He knew exactly how much money I had in my bank account, my retirement fund, and the limits on my credit cards. Hiring a hacker on the darknet, the doctor was aware of the amount of money I could afford to lose before we had met at the casino.

The green felt was smooth and inviting, just like Dr. Abbott's voice. I stared at the small ball rolling over the numbers in the roulette wheel until it finally landed, making most gamblers groan. I knew the house always wins, at least it did in the end... but what if I won instead? It was bound to happen from time to time, right?

I ended up losing all the money I had taken with me that night, being constantly pushed by my therapist to try again and again and again. Even when I won, I couldn't just turn around and leave with my earnings. I had to keep going, taking bigger and bigger risks.

I was glad I hadn't brought my credit cards with me because something in Dr. Abbott's bright blue eyes told me he would have kept pushing me until I was greatly in debt. Worse still, something in his soothing, velvety tone told me I would have agreed to it all.

Being around Dr. Abbott was like being on drugs, the good kind of drugs. The kind that made you feel like the king of the world. I felt thrilled as the date of our next session grew closer.

I no longer felt the need to lay in bed on my free days. I no longer felt miserable at work. Bit by bit, this man began to truly achieve what he had promised. Dr. Abbott was changing my life.

It was all part of his carefully planned formula of course. Everything he forced me to experience was intricately designed to keep me on his path. Beyond being a psychopath, he was a genius and genuinely believed that he was helping me find a cure for my depression.

We went bungee jumping, and when I refused to jump, he took it upon himself to push me off the ledge. At that moment, I felt like cursing him in as many languages as I could think of but after the adrenaline had filled my brain, I instantly became incredibly thankful.

Dr. Abbott kept pushing my limits further and further away from the lines I kept imagining in my head. Every single time he did, instead of leaving and quitting his program, I returned for more. I was eager, aching for the thrill only my moments by his side could provide.

Each time I began to panic, he found a way of either convincing me to give the experience a try regardless of my hesitance, or push me to follow his recommendation, whether I fully agreed to it or not.

Was it highly unconventional? Yes, and he had warned me it would be. Was it immoral for a shrink to be taking such liberties with his patient? Most likely, but every time I began to ponder the legality of his practices, I was drawn into a new and thrilling adventure, convinced to forgo rationality for excitement.

He knew exactly what to tell me. He knew exactly what to say. The profile he had created of me was that of a professional and he exploited his knowledge of me, the knowledge he acquired on the dark web, to cure me of my ailment.

"You can do this. All you have to do is jump," he would tell me every single time, and invariably, I would comply.

If his methods were becoming more and more extreme with every single activity, I was blind to this fact. All I could notice was how my life was no longer grey, how excited I was to get up in the morning, and how I looked forward to our sessions with increasing fervor.

I was like an addict, returning for more and more, begging for a session over the phone, thinking about our adventures as I laid in bed alone. Thinking about his recommendations even had me taking a shower, getting dressed, and going out to a bar one night. I hadn't done anything of the sort for years!

That night, I found a young, beautiful woman who was charmed by my newfound confidence and let me take her home. I hadn't been on a date for almost a year and yet I didn't even hesitate when asking her out.

I felt like a whole new man and I owed it all to Dr. Abbott. Being so grateful, I didn't even think of questioning his methods until it was far too late. I even came back to him after that particular incident with the car.

Incident. I shouldn't call it that. What he did to me that evening was outright suicidal and yet I came back to him the next session. He had told me we were going to try a brand new experience and I got in his car without a moment of hesitation.

I didn't think to ask where we were going, I was too naive to comprehend this trip would not be about the destination, but about the journey itself.

Doctor Abbott began heading toward a mountain road well-known for the frequency in which drivers traveling through it crashed. Some were lucky and were merely hospitalized for a few weeks. Others... well, let's say others aren't around to tell you about their accidents.

At first, I didn't think much of it. We were probably heading somewhere in the mountains. Perhaps we were going for a climb? I had discovered long before that nothing was impossible when it came to Doctor Abbott.

As he began taking the sharp curves with increasing speed and a careless disregard for our safety, I began to mildly panic, giving him a concerned look.

"Umm, Dr. Abbott?" I mumbled, trying to find my voice.

Sure, I was far more confident around almost everyone else in my life, including my boss, but when it came to my therapist, I had become increasingly compliant.

"Yes, Dylan?" he asked, a little smirk tugging at the edge of his lips.

That smirk worried me almost as much as the darkness in his eyes. The darkness I could no longer ignore.

Remember how I told you I could sense something off in his gaze whenever I stared at him through the corner of my eyes? Well, that had changed a while ago. I no longer had to be looking away to sense it.

It was as if the good doctor had finally let me peek at the true nature hiding behind the charismatic facade, and now I could sense the danger lurking so close to the surface I could almost reach out and touch it.

"I think we should slow down," I pleaded, my tone miserable and timid.

"You do?" he questioned, nonchalantly.

Everything about his tone seemed to imply he agreed, but his actions spoke otherwise. Doctor Abbott continued to accelerate instead, completely ignoring the brakes.

"We are going to crash!" I yelped, as we barely avoided a car speeding in the opposite lane.

He was driving in swift zig-zag movements by now, entering and exiting our lane with increasing disregard.

"And how does that make you feel?" he asked, trying to appear serious, yet I could clearly sense a sadistic pleasure in his every word.

"Horrified! Please stop!" I pleaded, but didn't dare move an inch, too afraid I'd make things worse... if that was even possible.

"Doesn't it make you feel excited?" He was speaking as if we were sitting across from each other in his comfortable office instead of facing near-certain death on a mountain road.

"No!"

"Don't lie to me," he barked.

It was then that he crossed lanes once more. There was a car ahead of us, moving closer and closer with each passing second. The sound of the other driver's horns flooded my head.

"Does it make you feel excited?"

"Yes!" I admitted in a panic, holding onto my seat and preparing for the worse.

We were going to die, and there was nothing I could do to stop it!

At the last second, Abbott veered the steering wheel back to the right, dodging the incoming car by inches. I could barely hear the cursing of the other driver or the frantic horns any longer. All I could hear was the beating of my own heart drumming away in my ears.

I had almost forgotten how to breathe and it took me a few moments to compose myself enough to inhale and exhale properly. It was more than enough time for Doctor Abbott to park at a lookout point by the edge of the road.

"I think your therapy is almost over, my dear friend," Doctor Abbott said soothingly as if we hadn't been seconds away from sure death.

"I'm very proud of you, young man."

That was all I needed to hear. Instead of frowning and yelling at him, suddenly I was smiling, feeling like I had overcome a paralyzing phobia thanks to his wonderful methods. The voice in my head that warned me about the darkness in his blue eyes was fading away with concerning speed.

At the time, I truly believed that would be as far as my therapist would take his insane experiment. That was it, there was nowhere to go from there, right? Soon I would be cured and would be able to live a healthy, happy life.

How naive I was.

By then, I had gotten used to grabbing a cup of coffee almost every morning at a coffee shop close to my job, and Doctor Abbott knew it all too well. How could he not, when I talked to him repeatedly about the cute barista I was trying to find the courage to ask out on a date?

Of course, the doctor was not just aware of my morning ritual because I had mentioned it. He was tracking the GPS on my phone. Dr. Abbott knew where I was at all times.

I was in line, waiting for my coffee, staring at the full lips and green eyes of the pretty girl brewing the drinks when I heard it, a loud roar coming from my right as if someone was trying to scare me silly.

Jumping away from something swinging towards my head, I barely managed to dodge the attack. I'm not embarrassed to admit I was terrified by the sudden turn of events. Much to my dismay, I realized I had almost been struck with the butt of a gun.

My attacker was a man in his forties, a full head taller than me and twice as big. He had tried to hit me and at the time, I did not comprehend how it was possible he had failed. He was clearly built to hurt men with far more wits and dexterity than me, and yet I had been able to jump away from his attack.

People began rushing away from my assailant, and I tried to do the same, but the rough man followed behind me with surprising speed. The hitman aimed his gun at me. I could hear the panicked screams of those who ran out the door. I could not run to the door. I was completely paralyzed with fear, feeling like a deer caught in the headlights.

I could not possibly know this was all meant to be a test. Doctor Abbott had planned it, hiring the assassin himself, certain that this would be my final test, the way to gain back my life for good.

Dr. Abbott reached into the darkness of the internet to provide the proof he needed to verify his methods. My cure for depression.

The ultimate adrenaline rush could only come from one thing, fighting for one's own life.

A dark web hitman was hired to find me at the coffee shop and end my life. The doctor provided photos for the assassin but in an odd twist, did not provide the tracking for my phone. He would later confess that he didn't think it would be "fair" for my potential killer to have it.

I felt it, a painful burning sensation that began at my shoulder yet spread all over my body in a matter of seconds. It was a pain unlike anything I had experienced before.

Blood poured down my chest, and I knew I had been shot. This man had given me time to dodge him once, but whatever advantage I had an instant ago, was long gone now. I was going to die.

Just as suddenly as I had felt the piercing pain fill me completely, I reacted. I had never done anything of the sort before, but this was do or die, and apparently I was not ready for the latter.

I had never experienced such adrenaline before, not even when Dr. Abbott drove straight toward an oncoming car. This was it. This was the pivotal moment of my life and if I didn't act the way I should, it would be the last moment as well.

It was almost as if I was watching myself move from outside my body, jumping over the counter, grabbing a glass coffee pot filled to the brim with steaming liquid and finally crouching away from my assailant's view.

I lurked there, my heart beating so fast I was certain my attacker could hear it a mile away. I held my breath and waited for him to move closer. It was a violent, sudden movement, as I smashed the coffee pot against the side of his head.

I felt it shatter to pieces, pouring hot coffee all over his face and body, making him scream and tumble back. He tried to aim at me and shoot, while screaming obscenities at me, but the bullet hit the ceiling instead.

In the distance, the police sirens were approaching, but I didn't rush outside. I couldn't. My assailant was on the floor and my single thought was the overwhelming urge to take charge of my life. I jumped at him, ready to attack him and ready to wrestle the gun out of his hands.

I was ready to murder him.

He was, as I would find out later, a professional. He knew what he was doing and even while shrieking in pain, he was still twice as big as I was. The kick he gave me sent me flying to the floor, gasping for air and grabbing at my chest. It gave him the chance he needed to escape.

I'm certain if the police weren't arriving, he would have shot me right then and there. He would have ended me but didn't have enough time. So he ran. He ran and got away, much to my horror. The intellectual author of my attempted murder was far easier to find, though.

*   *   *

"You can't arrest me! Don't you realize I'm a genius?!" Dr. Abbott would protest days later when the police apprehended him.

"He graduated from the program! He took charge of his life! Don't you see I'm his savior?!"

The trial wasn't long, but it was indeed highly publicized. Everyone seemed to have an opinion on the matter. Dr. Abbott swore over and over that his intention was never to harm me. He knew I'd fight back, that I'd defend my life and finally understand its worth.

Some people called him insane, others called him a visionary. Whatever the truth was, he was found guilty but amazingly was only forced to pay a hefty sum to avoid jail time.

Rumors that he knew some high powered people within the justice department persisted when the verdict came without any jail time. I knew that whatever power he had over them had come from his dealings on the darknet. As a victim of his methods, I'm sure he used the same programs he used to find information about me.

He would never be allowed to practice medicine again, but I knew he'd find a way around it. How could he not? Even when he was being found guilty, I could sense that dark satisfaction in his eyes.

His dark, dangerous eyes. Doctor Abbott disappeared from my life just as suddenly as he had arrived, yet the imprint he left behind marks me to this very day.

If he could find my medical records, gain access to my bank accounts, and hire an assassin to kill me then there was no doubt that Dr. Abbott could get a fake ID. I imagined him sitting in a small European town with a new name, a new medical license, and a new target.

He did cure me, despite his wretched ways. My life has been brimming with positivity, even after the attack and the lawsuit. I don't need to work any longer. The judge was very generous in providing me with compensatory damages for my trauma.

During the sentencing, he addressed me directly, saying he hoped I would live a comfortable, safe life away from predators like Doctor Abbott. He wished I had learned my lesson.

And I genuinely have. He probably meant not to be so trusting, but that's not the case. I have learned that life is not worth living without a little bit of risk… or a lot of it for that matter. Dr. Abbott saved my life by trying to take it from me.

I used some of the money from the lawsuit and followed the doctor into the darker reaches of the internet. In a short time, packages began to arrive at my house. A pistol with the serial numbers removed, some body armor, a dozen burner phones, and a multitude of ID's that spanned the globe.

My last act on the grid was to delve into the bowels of the internet and place a very healthy bounty on my own head. The first person to kill me by any means would become a millionaire.

As I pack my bags for the third time this month ready to go on the run again, sensing death breathing down my neck, with another bullet wound to heal from, I know in my heart that I have never felt more alive.

<u>Feed an Author, Leave a Review!</u>

Thank you for taking the time to read my book. I hope that you have enjoyed my stories as much as I have enjoyed writing them. Reviews make the world of an author go round and I treasure each and every one. If you liked my work, please take a moment to leave a review. It doesn't have to be long or fancy, just a few kind words will do. It takes many hours, dollars, and a great deal of effort to write and release a book and it gives me tremendous satisfaction whenever I receive a review. Thank you for your support!

Follow, Like, and Subscribe!!!

Follow me on Social Media or sign up for my newsletter to stay up to date with my upcoming work, special discounts, and even the opportunity to become a beta reader or a member of my ARC Team!

Newsletter:

https://mailchi.mp/2782f017142c/jtwithelder

Facebook:

https://www.facebook.com/j.t.withelder

Instagram:

https://www.instagram.com/j.t.withelder/

About the Author

Justin Toby Withelder, or J.W. to his closest friends, was born, raised, and lives in rural Pennsylvania with the love of his life, Carrie, and his two children.

Taking an interest in reading and storytelling at a young age, and was further encouraged by his uncles, Paul and Harry, who frequently gave books as gifts for birthdays and at Christmas.

He has been writing both long and short stories as a hobby for many years in the science fiction, horror, and thriller genres. Pulling inspiration from his favorite authors, Stephen King and Michael Crichton, and television shows like "The Twilight Zone", Justin prefers to focus on the terror of the unknown rather than an explainable creature or phenomenon.

He is an engineer by trade but prefers to spend his time outdoors whenever possible. He enjoys hunting, fishing, hiking, and camping. He and his wife also enjoy visiting theme parks, specifically to ride roller coasters. They plan to travel the world to ride the biggest and fastest coasters.

Tales from the Dark Web

First paperback edition May 2020

ISBN 978-1-6945-4860-3

Made in the USA
Monee, IL
21 November 2024

70690072R00121